Bill Condon's novel *Confessions of a Liar, Thief and Failed Sex God* was the winner of the inaugural Young Adult Fiction prize in the 2010 Prime Minister's Literary Awards. His other novels for young adults include *No Worries*, which was an Honour Book in the CBCA awards for older readers in 2006, and was also shortlisted for the NSW Premier's Literary Awards. *Dogs* was an Honour Book in the CBCA awards for older readers in 2001.

Bill lives on the south coast of NSW with his wife, the author Dianne Bates. Before writing for children and young adults, Bill worked as a journalist on a suburban newspaper. He has written non-fiction, short stories, poetry and plays.

For more information about Bill and his books go to www.enterprisingwords.com

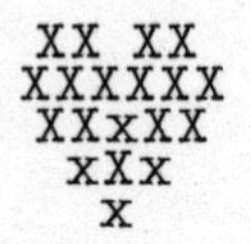

~~A Straight Line to My~~ Heart

Other books by Bill Condon

Give Me Truth

Dare Devils

No Worries

From Hero to Zero

A Straight Line to My HEART

Bill Condon

First published in 2011

Allen & Unwin
83 Alexander Street, Crows Nest NSW 2065, Australia
Phone (61 2) 8425 0100
Fax (61 2) 9906 2218
Email info@allenandunwin.com
Web www.allenandunwin.com

A Cataloguing-in-Publication entry is available from the National Library of Australia: www.trove.nla.gov.au

ISBN 978 174237 730 8

Teachers' notes available from www.allenandunwin.com

Design by Bruno Herfst
Set in 11.5 pt Caslon Classico
Printed in Australia by McPherson's Printing Group

10 9 8 7 6 5 4 3 2 1

The paper in this book is FSC certified. FSC promotes environmentally responsible, socially beneficial and economically viable management of the world's forests.

With love to my family,
and especially to Di,
and also to my very first editor,
Larry Rivera,
who taught me so much.

CHAPTER 1

THERE'S NOTHING QUITE AS good as folding up into a book and shutting the world outside. If I pick the right one I can be beautiful, or fall in love, or live happily ever after. Maybe even all three.

If you can't get a boy, get a book, that's my motto.

Here I am in Gungee Creek Library. It's tiny and cramped but it has ceiling fans and the bus stop is only a short walk away. I have twenty-five minutes to wait for my ride home. That's plenty of time for me to visit an old friend named *Wuthering Heights.*

It's all so sad. Catherine died two hours after the birth of her daughter. Just like my mum. And Emily Brontë, the author, died not long after finishing the story.

Young Cathy is asked why she loves Edgar Linton. She dodges around before at last admitting: 'I love the ground under his feet, and the air over his head, and every word he says . . .'

On and on she goes with this romantic drivel. It's too much, Cathy. But still, I wouldn't mind feeling that way about someone, especially if he felt the same way about me. I wouldn't go for Edgar, though; tall and windswept Heathcliff for me, every time. And there wouldn't be any tragic misunderstandings if we hooked up. It would be . . .

'Scuse me.'

A guy stands in front of me.

'Yes?'

'Sorry to interrupt.' He grins for no reason. This is not a promising sign. 'You don't know where there's a toilet around here, do you?'

He's large and slouchy, like a vertical beanbag.

'Go out the door. Take a left. Take another left. Toilet.'

'Must have gone right past it. What was it again? Take a left and then . . .?'

'Two lefts. One. Two. It's the second one.'

'Got it.'

'You can't go wrong. Come back if you do.'

'Ta. I'll go check it out.'

'Yes. Do that.'

He gives me a toothy smile then holds and holds the

pose as though he's being photographed for *Village Idiot Weekly*, before at last he turns and lopes away.

I feel like writing a stern note to the librarian.

Dear Ms Dombkins,
I strongly suggest the library overhaul its security procedures. Today my sanctuary was violated by a Big Foot!
Outraged, of Gungee Creek.

I try to slip back to *Wuthering Heights*.

'Oh, these bleak winds, and bitter northern skies, and impassable roads . . .'

Oh, forget it. One minute ago I had no trouble imagining myself battling along on the frozen heath, but now an invader has trampled all over the mood. I've left *Wuthering Heights* and I'm stuck back here in the boiling heat of Gungee.

Damn.

He was wearing red shorts with a blue stripe. So he plays for Tarwyn, forty-five minutes drive north of here. He's more hulk than hunk, but I have to admit he's got a cute smile. About my age or just a bit more, probably blown in for the day to have a game at the oval tomorrow. The Tarwyn crew often arrives a day early. My guess is their coach likes to have some of his gorillas stroll around town to intimidate the Gunners. Smart move. This guy looked like he eats smaller footy players for breakfast.

I kinda want to see him again, if only to do a little exploring. Who knows – I might even like what I find. Only problem is, exploring takes bravery and I'm fresh out. It's easier to hunch down and bury my head in some musty pages, while trying to watch the library exit sign out of the corner of my eye. In a few minutes he should be on his way.

I wait and wait. Where's he got to? Maybe he's pushing on the toilet door instead of pulling on it. He might never get out of there.

Uh-oh. Here he comes.

'Scuse me.'

I look up and there he is.

'You didn't get lost, did you?' I ask.

'Nuh. No trouble at all. Your directions were spot on.'

'Good . . . so you're probably looking for the exit. Out that door.'

'I know. I was looking for you.'

He's grinning again.

Ms Dombkins, where are you? Help!

'Me?'

'Yeah, I didn't introduce myself before; was in a bit of a rush. When you gotta go–'

He puts out his hand – I say a silent prayer that he washed it – and reluctantly give him mine.

'Davey Peters.'

His handshake is almost gentle. That's a trick serial killers use to lure you into a false sense of security.

'And you'd be?'

No, no. Wait. I've had second thoughts. I'm no explorer. I'm not interested in knowing you.

Look at you. Now look at me. What is wrong with this picture?

Both of us!

He's a bumble-headed sleepwalker, twice my size.

And I'm just an ordinary girl – *too* ordinary. No boy ever notices me.

Tell him that. Tell him!

I always talk to myself but I hardly ever listen.

'Tiff.'

'Ohhh, Tiff,' he says, pretending he understands, when it's obvious to me that he doesn't. Looks like I have to explain it.

'Short for Tiffany. Tiff is what I usually get – Tiffy sometimes – basically I'll answer to any name that starts with a T.'

Oh God, now I'm grinning. I'm as bad as him. And I'm babbling, too. I'm nervous, that's the problem. It's a natural reaction when you're confronted by a Big Foot who won't take his eyes off you.

Look at something else. The library has lots of pretty pictures on the wall. Stare at them, not me.

'Tiff like in *Breakfast at Tiffany's*,' he says. 'Right?'

I couldn't be more shocked.

'Um . . . yes, that's right – it's an old movie.'

'Is it? Don't watch much TV. I've only heard of the book – got it at home. I bought it 'cause Truman Capote wrote it. I was stoked by *In Cold Blood.* He wrote that, too. You read it?'

'No.'

'Aw, you gotta. It rocks.'

I look away as if I've been suddenly distracted by something out the window. It's my version of the pause button. There's a lot of information to process. Here's a boy my own age; he shakes my hand, he talks to me – not just to ask directions to the toilet – and he reads books.

Heathcliff?

'Oops. Almost forgot why I came back in to see you.'

Those words hit my brain and just reverberate – he came back to see me! I try hard not to let my feelings show, but there's nothing I can do about the wave of redness that engulfs my face. I so hope he's colour blind.

'Um . . . so why did you come back?'

'Raffle tickets.' He takes out a book of them. 'The Blues are raising money for equipment. You want to buy some? Three for five bucks. Top prizes.'

CHAPTER 2

As I sit at the bus stop I see Mrs Muir's sunflowers. Her front garden is infested with them; tall and vibrant. To me they're a symbol of sheer happiness. That is really rubbing my nose in it. Well, I've had enough and I'm not going to take it anymore!

Even as I stomp over there, the evil thought swelling up in me, I tell myself I can't do this. I won't.

Another voice rages.

I hate that boy! I hate me! I am so incredibly stupid!

A sunflower leans over the fence, smiling.

How dare you!

I rip off its head and throw it in the gutter.

The smart thing to do is to keep on going. Walk away quickly and no one will know what I've done.

But I can't move because my eyes are locked on the slowly opening front door – locked on Mrs Muir.

'I'm sorry.' My tiny voice sounds so pathetically lame, but I've got still more lameness for her.

'I never do this sort of thing. I like sunflowers. I was just angry about something – nothing to do with you or the flower. I'm really, really sorry.'

'Oh, you *are* upset. Well, never mind.' Mrs Muir comes closer to me. 'Goodness, we all get cross. The main thing is: did it make you feel any better?'

'No. Yes. Maybe. A little bit.'

'Would you like to do another one? There's more out the back, too. You go for your life, dear. I don't mind at all – they need a good pruning.'

She's an old, close-to-the-ground, jelly-belly woman with bald patches showing through her wispy grey hair. It doesn't seem like she's got a lot going for her, but she's still smiling. Been around the sunflowers too long, I'd say.

'No thanks, Mrs Muir, but I'll keep it in mind for another time.' I open the gate and walk into her yard. 'Are you going to the game tomorrow?'

'Oh yes. I always get along to support our boys.'

'Thought so. Please take these to make up for the flower.'

I put them in her hand. 'Raffle tickets. They're drawn at half time. All paid for. Top prizes.'

'What a lovely thought.'

She wraps her arms around me and holds me like I'm hers.

CHAPTER 3

On the bus home I ring my best friend Kayla to tell her about my strange visitor.

'What a creep! Hitting on you – at the library of all places – and then trying to sell you raffle tickets. I would have told him where to go.'

'Thanks, but boys don't actually hit on me, Kayla. I am not exactly flavour of the month.'

'Yeah, that's true.'

'You didn't have to agree so quickly.'

'Aw, Tiff, I'm sorry. It could be different, if a boy ever got to know you . . .'

Kayla and boys go together like chocolate and pimples. She can have her pick of any guy she wants. She's friends with Jarrod and Ryan and once she almost agreed to Gabriel Bronkowski's suggestion that they live together. But then she realised that Gabe meant 'live together with him and his mum'. Pass.

Mostly Kayla can't be bothered because she thinks boys are too possessive and she likes her freedom, doesn't want to get tied down to just one person. As for me, I wouldn't mind, not if he was the right person; wouldn't mind at all.

'This guy sounds like a tool,' she says.

'No, he wasn't that bad – I was just being naïve, as usual.'

'Don't defend him. I know you, Tiff. He must have made some impression on you, or else you wouldn't have told me about him. I bet you got your hopes up – I bet you were hurt.'

'Okay, but it was my own fault. He was being friendly, that's all.'

'Of course he was. So he could sell you raffle tickets.'

I know she's right.

'Please tell me you didn't buy any. That would be really tragic if you did.'

'Not a chance. Are you joking? I still have *some* pride.'

CHAPTER 4

I STROLL INTO THE KITCHEN. Bull's making lunch. He's actually no relation to me, though secretly I look on him as my big brother, sometimes even my dad. When I needed a father for parent–teacher nights, Bull was there; if I fell out of a tree he'd run to catch me. He usually dropped me, but at least he tried; he's my full-time bodyguard and chauffeur, and, when I was thirteen and feeling depressed after spending too long in front of a mirror, he was the one I asked – 'Do you think I'm pretty?'

'No, mate,' he said, 'I wouldn't call you pretty at all. No way. You're beautiful.'

It's still near the top of my all-time favourite lies.

I don't tell him how I feel about him because he'd get a swelled head. And one thing Bull doesn't need is a bigger head.

Nor do I tell him about Big Foot. I figure it's best to forget him and his stupid raffle tickets.

Reggie's sitting at the table looking more despondent than usual. His face has as many lines as the state rail system, and though he still has some hair, most of it is poking out of his ears and nose. Hair on the head is too ordinary anyway. If I think of Bull as my dad, then Reggie has to be my grandfather. He's way old and he's kind to me like a grandfather should be, but if I call him Pops or Gramps he goes right off. Says it makes him feel 'like a relic'. So to me he's always Reggie.

Our family tree is kind of twisty-turny. Reggie and his wife, Nell, were friends with my mum's only sister, Debbie. When Mum died, Auntie Debbie couldn't look after me herself, and there were no other volunteers for the job, so she asked Reggie and Nell if they'd take me. I think it was only a stop-gap fostering thing at first, but I was probably a really cute baby, so I stayed.

Nell was married before, when she was a lot younger, but it didn't last long. One dark and stormy night she left her husband and moved in with Reggie. Her little boy was part of the package deal. That was Bull. He was twenty-two by the time I joined the family.

- - + - -

'What's up?' I ask Reggie.

'Eughhh.'

That's the noise a snarl makes.

'As bad as that, huh?'

'Yeah, Tiffy. It's that bloke over there.' He points to Bull to make sure I know who he means. There's no one else in the kitchen so I could probably have guessed. 'He's got no respect.'

'You're not wrong.' I pat Reggie's back as I wander past. 'He's a lowlife, all right.'

'Who you callin' a lowlife?' That's the unmistakable, deep-down-in-the-dungeon voice of Bull.

And then I'm next to him, leaning in like a pesky calf pushing up against a tree. If I didn't annoy him he'd think there was something wrong.

'Get out of it, you!'

I take both barrels of his steely gaze as he tries to look mean. It only makes me laugh.

He used to be a boxer: Wild Bull Bennett. Gave that up years ago and joined the police. His mates don't need a battering ram when they have Bull with them; they send him charging first though the door every time. Just the look of him scares the crooks half to death. But he doesn't scare me. It's the other way around, as it should be.

'What's cookin', Greg-ory?' He hates it when I call him that.

'Bacon, tomatoes, scrambled eggs; food for the gods. But Wolfie's gunna be havin' your share if you're not careful, Tiff-a-ny.'

Ouch. I hate being called that, too. It's hard to score any points when you know each other's weaknesses so well.

I pull up a chair next to Reggie.

'What's all this about him giving you no respect?'

Bull jumps in before Reggie can open his mouth. 'His usual garbage. Yesterday he felt a bit off-colour so now he decides he's on his way out. Tells me he's going to leave me the Falcon. Whoopy-do. Only been working on it ten years and he still can't get it on the road.'

'But I will. You can put money on it. And by the way, I felt more than off-colour, boy. I tell yer, there's somethin' wrong with me throat. I can feel it.'

'Not another tea leaf is it?'

'Aw, give it a rest. When are you gunna forget that? It was ages ago.'

Only last year, actually. Reggie was convinced he had cancer because he had a black spot on his tongue – he switched to tea bags after the doctor told him it was a tea leaf.

'Look,' Bull says, 'if you're really concerned, go and see Anna. She'll put your mind at ease.'

'I'll save me money, thanks. Already diagnosed meself, anyway. I'm cactus.'

'Cactus? Right. Great work, there, Doc. I'm glad you're not my bloody doctor.'

'Well what do you want me to say? That's how I feel.'

'You're a misery guts, that's what's wrong with you. Ever since Rupes died you've been like this.'

'He was me best mate, Bull.'

'He was a rabbit.'

'Still me best mate.'

'You'll always have me,' I say.

'And don't think I'm not grateful.' Reggie manages a craggy smile. 'But you'll be leavin' here one day. Sure as eggs.'

I wish I could say it wasn't true, but I know it is. Soon as I can I'm getting out of Gungee. I'll keep on going until I find where I'm meant to be.

Nell died when I was five so I was raised by these two boofy blokes. It was a challenge for all of us, but we've scraped through. No, that's not fair – we've sailed through, had the best time. Still, I can't stay their little girl forever, even though it's very tempting.

'I'll be in your life, no matter what,' I tell him, which isn't a lie – it just might be from a distance. 'And you've got Wolfie.'

'Nah. The Wolf's your mutt now – I'm leavin' her to you

in me will. Got it all sorted; I'm packed and ready to go.'

I'm really fascinated to know what sort of things he's packed in preparation for dying – how would you know what the weather was going to be like? But before I get around to asking, Bull interrupts.

'Better unpack, old fella. You're not going anywhere. Don't even think about it.'

'Sooner or later I need to get the arrangements settled.'

'You and yer flamin' arrangements.'

'Now you remember this – when I go you can burn me up in the incinerator out the backyard and then bung me ashes in the garbage bin. Green one if yer like, so I get recycled. That's me last wish and testament.'

'Wait a second.' Bull pauses to flip over the bacon. 'Okay, now listen. When you go you're gettin' a proper funeral with all the bells and whistles. And I don't want to hear any arguments.'

'No one would turn up to see me off.'

'Of course they would – they'd want to make sure you didn't change your mind.'

'Funerals are too sad.'

'Sad? You're havin' yourself on, mate. No one's gunna be sad over you. They'll be dancing in the street.'

'All right then, have it your way; but whatever you do, I've got instructions.'

'Thought you might.'

'There are only two things.'

'Go on.'

'One: If anyone feels the urge to get up and say what a good fella I was, they can put a sock in it. If they haven't told me when I'm alive, then it's too late when I've carked it.'

'Got it.'

'Two: I want you to have a party. Be sure you have sparklers – they were always me favourite – no crackers 'cause they'd scare the Wolf. Fire up the barbie, play the old Beatles' records, some Elvis, sing and dance, have a beer, tell some jokes – you get the idea?'

'Think so, Reggie.'

'I hope you do, because if I catch anyone howlin', I'll come back and haunt yers!'

CHAPTER 5

AFTER LUNCH REGGIE GOES into his room and shuts the door – probably to do some last-minute packing – so I get to talk to Bull on his own.

I ask the most important question first. 'Is he really sick?'

We're sitting on the front verandah, which we also call the Oval Office because across the road is Gungee Oval, where Bull and the Gunners have so often covered themselves in disgrace.

'He quit the smokes today, Tiff. Been puffing away for sixty years, feels somethin' in his throat, gives it up in one day – bang.'

That bothers me too.

'Smokers quit all the time,' I say, playing it down. 'You'll see. Give him a couple of days and he'll light up again.'

Bull stares into the hazy distance as though the right words are out there somewhere and all he has to do is claim them as his own. Sometimes it gets so quiet in Gungee you can hear conversations from a hundred years ago breathing on a gust of wind. Least it feels that way now as I wait for Bull to say something. But finally he just shakes his head and shrugs, and lets it go at that.

I hear a scratchy sound at the screen door and the tiny but insistent whimper that belongs to Wolfie. She's a greyhound, a retired racer, fawn and white and beautiful.

'Yes, you can come out.' I open the door for her. She wags her tail to thank me and toddles onto the verandah.

'Don't you get up here,' snarls Bull. 'This seat is taken.'

Wolfie clambers up next to him and gets the pat on the head that Bull always gives her, despite his protests. She's got him figured out.

She waits till I sit before she makes herself comfortable, turns all the way round – once, twice – flops down and sighs as if she's had a really hard day, and stretches out full-length, draping herself over my lap so I can rub her soft, warm coat.

CHAPTER 6

ZOE BREEZES IN, FULL of smiles: Bull's girlfriend. It's always real with her, like she's honestly glad to see me. She's the same with Reggie, though he doesn't exactly throw out the welcome mat in return. I think he likes her, deep down, but he's got his castle to defend, his home. He's set in his ways. He doesn't make any big speeches about it; doesn't carry on and thump the table. But every so often after Zoe's been over I'll hear him mumbling to himself about 'females takin' over the joint'.

Zoe gets this. She doesn't poke her head in here all that often, and her Reggie-pecks-to-the-cheek are quick and painless – like shooting a tranquiliser dart into a bear. She takes it slow and easy with me, too. Doesn't try to push friendship at me – just as well, because I'd only push it right back at her.

Bull left home when he was nineteen. He had girlfriends then; lived with a couple of them for a while, went to Hawaii with one. When Nell died he moved back in, to look after Reggie, I suppose, and me. I remember lots of Saturday nights and dates with girls; him trying on shirt after shirt – I used to tease him about it. But I don't remember him being as happy as he is now, with Zoe.

She's no girly-girl. Not into fashion or make-up. With her it's jeans and plenty of soap and hot water. She's middle-of-the-road pretty but will never stop any traffic; medium height and sturdy build; and her blonde hair's all business, cropped short and straight. One look tells you she's tough; doesn't take backward steps. But she melts around Bull. He's the same with her.

'She's got him under the thumb,' Reggie says, 'and he doesn't even know it. It's pitiful. Next thing yer know he'll be buyin' her flowers.'

I don't think that's ever going to happen, but I'd love to see it. They sit on the front steps together swapping cop stories – she's in the job, too – and it isn't long before he says something that gets her laughing. Zoe is the kind of person you wouldn't want to have next to you in a funny movie. When she laughs she doesn't care what it sounds like or how loud it is, and I'm guessing she wouldn't care what anyone else thinks. Embarrassment City, that's where she lives.

Back inside again and all of us are gathered around the TV. Wolfie meanders over to say hello and Zoe drops to the floor to play a game – growling and hissing like the big bad dog Wolfie doesn't know how to be. The Wolf retreats to the tickle-position, flat on her back, legs up in the air.

I wouldn't go against Reggie and actively encourage Zoe to move in, but I think she and I would do okay together. If nothing else she could help me in my never-ending campaign. Some people want to save the rivers or save the whales, even save the entire planet – I just want to keep the toilet seat down.

She might also be able to civilise Bull, or at least curb some of his bogan behaviour. Let's not beat about the bush. I'm talking gas. When Bull gets together with his footy mates and they've downed a few beers it's a competition to see who can blast the biggest hole in the ozone layer. And they think they're being witty. Somehow I don't think Zoe would appreciate their attempts at humour.

But regardless of whether she could tame Bull, she'd be fun to have around, and when I got to know her better we could talk long into the night about nothing, and everything. I'd really like that.

All that's a long way off, and it may never happen at all, but for now we've got the afternoon together, and that look in her eyes tells me she's in a playful mood.

'You want to watch a movie with us, Reggie?' she asks.

'Depends what it is. I'm a busy man, yer know. Always something needs doin' around the place.'

Zoe has put me up to this. So, with a straight face, I tell him, 'It's a Western. Some guy called John Wayne. Have you heard of him?'

Reggie looks like he's about to launch into a cartwheel.

'The old John Wayne, eh? Never made a crook movie in his life, that bloke. I seen just about every one he did but I could watch 'em all again. Even Nell liked him, and she really wasn't all that fond of Westerns. Yeah, I'll watch that with yers.'

But now Reggie takes a closer look at our faces. He sees Bull straining to keep his mouth closed for fear a laugh will come tumbling out. He sees Zoe try to look him in the eye, only to turn away when she realises he can see too much. And probably the thing that really gives it away, is when I giggle.

'You cheeky buggers. You haven't got a John Wayne at all, have yers?'

'Sorry, Reggie.' I put my arms around his waist, my head on his shoulder. 'Are you still talking to me?'

'Nuh. You've done yer dash with me. The lots of yers. That's it. Finished. Hooroo.'

'Don't be like that, Reggie. Talk to me. Pleeeaase.'

It's a game we play. He acts tough and I act soft.

'Aw, all right then. Might as well. Got no one else ter talk to . . . now what are yers really gunna watch?'

'This.' Zoe hands him the DVD case.

'*Eclipse*,' he says, holding the case at arm's length to read the title. 'Don't suppose it's a documentary?'

Apart from *Dr Phil* – he loves *Dr Phil* – the only shows he likes to watch on TV are very old movies and documentaries.

'No, sorry, Reggie. It's about vampires.'

'Yeah? I don't mind the occasional vampire.'

'It's got romance, too,' Zoe adds. 'Loads of it.'

'That's a pity.'

'There's even kissing,' I say. 'It won't be as good as John Wayne.'

'That's for sure, luv. All Big John ever did was punch blokes and shoot 'em. Family entertainment. You can't go wrong with that formula. You never had to fast-forward any of his stuff. '

'So you're not going to watch it with us?' asks Bull, trying to sound disappointed.

'Well I wasn't goin' to, but I'd hate to let yer down.'

'Don't worry about us, mate. If you're busy, you just go, we'll understand.'

'No, no. You twisted me arm. Switch her on.'

I expect Reggie to last about ten minutes, but he stays the distance, kind of. He's wide awake and on the edge of his seat when the vampires are fighting.

'This isn't too bad at all,' he says. 'I reckon I could be a fan.'

But when the movie goes quiet, apart from squelchy kissing noises and heavy breathing, he gets up to go to the toilet. 'No, no, don't pause it for me – I'll survive'. And when he comes back and there's more kissing, he goes to sleep with his mouth open, and dribbles.

'I'm not asleep,' he insists when he catches me looking at him, 'just restin' me eyes, that's all.'

Wolfie joins us, too. She prefers the commercials to movies, but if someone's there to rub her belly, she'll watch anything. Wolfie is very much like Reggie. She sleeps a lot, she's lovable, and she's desperate for company.

The credits start to roll. And Reggie wakes up, coughing. I've listened to his cough first thing every morning for years. Usually he hacks away for a minute or so and then there's quiet again. This isn't like that. He sits up, holding his throat, coughing and coughing.

'Are you okay?'

'Can I get you some water?'

'Reggie?'

His fingers dig into the sides of the chair, his eyes wide and scared. The coughing rips through him, flings him forward and back. Zoe has her mobile in her hand ready to press triple-o.

'Reggie – I'll get help.'

'No. No.' He gasps it, a hanky to his mouth. 'I'm all right.'

Gradually the coughing eases and my heart stops pounding. He manages to get to his feet. Bull and Zoe hang on to him but he pulls away.

'Don't fuss. It's nothin' to worry over. I just need a glass of water. I swallowed the wrong way, that's all. Let me catch me breath. I'll be right.'

Then I see the blood on his lips.

CHAPTER 7

BULL INSISTS HE'S GOING to call a doctor. Reggie insists right back at him.

'No you bloody will not. I don't need no doctor.' He retreats into his room and slams the door behind him. 'Let a man have some peace, will yer?'

Bull: 'Stubborn bugger. I oughta just drag him into the car and make him see Anna.'

Zoe: 'No, we should back off; let him settle down for a while.'

Me: 'Reggie. I'm coming in.'

When there's no reply, I twist the doorknob . . .

'Before yer start on me, Tiffy, don't waste yer breath. I'm not seein' a doctor.'

'Can I at least sit on the bed? I won't say anything. I just want to be here with you.'

It's so dark with the curtains drawn I could believe I was in a cave, if not for a clock banging out the seconds.

Reggie finally answers, his voice caught somewhere between sad and strong.

'A man doesn't deserve a girl like you.'

'Does that mean I can sit down?'

'I could never say no to you, Tiffy, you know that. Twirled me around yer finger from when you were a little kid. Yeah, go ahead.'

He taps the side of the bed and I take his hand in mine.

'Don't know what all that coughin' was about, but it knocked the stuffin' out of me. I'm worn out now.'

'Then go with it, Reggie. Close your eyes.'

'Don't think I can sleep. I feel a bit rattled. A smoke might settle me down but I don't want one. Can't remember the last time I felt like that.'

'How about I read to you?'

'Nah. I think I'm past bedtime stories.'

'No you're not.'

I switch on the light so I can see his bookshelf. I know exactly which one to choose.

'Your favourite poet, Reggie?'

He looks at the cover and nods.

'Banjo Paterson, eh?'

'So I can read to you?'

'I wouldn't say no. But I can tell yer now, I won't be able to sleep.'

Reggie used to read these poems to me when I was little.

I start: '*On the Outer Barcoo–*'

And Reggie joins in –

'*Where the churches are few–*'

'Shh! I'm the reader. You're the audience.'

'Aw. Righto. Carry on.'

I read it to the end.

'It's a good 'un that.'

'Let's see what else is here. How about–'

'No, Tiffy. I've had enough for now, thanks. You run along. I'll be fine.'

I don't feel good about leaving him, not yet, so I go over to his record player, turn it down low, and play 'Let It Be'.

He closes his eyes and breathes out slowly, letting go of any remaining tension.

Our house has heard that song so often it's a wonder it just doesn't come on automatically when we go inside. It's Reggie's all-time fave, and his philosophy of life. For nearly anything that went wrong with me as I grew up – school or boys or a mortal fear of swimming costumes that made me look like Shrek's hideous sister – 'Let It Be' was Reggie's answer. And when the message finally got through to me – when I stopped worrying and started going with the flow

– everything gradually worked itself out, just like he said it would.

I'm about to play the record for a second time when I notice that Reggie is making little whistly snores.

I creep out of the room and back to Bull and Zoe.

'How is he?'

'Zonked.'

Bull nods. 'Kayla rang. Said you were going to help her babysit tonight.'

'I was, but I can't now. Did you tell her?'

'Nah. Told her you'd be there.'

'But I can't, Bull. I have to stay home, in case something happens.'

'Nothing's going to happen.'

'How do you know?'

He glances at Zoe. It's that tag-team thing that old married couples do. With one look he passes the question to her, and she answers.

'We see a lot of sick people in our job, Tiff. Old people, especially. You get to know how bad it is. Reggie's okay for now. He'll soon let us know if he's not. We'll be right here – won't we, Bull?'

'For sure,' he says. 'So you go see Kayla like you planned. There could be other times when you're needed here, but we got it covered tonight.'

CHAPTER 8

KAYLA AND I BOTH live in Abercrombie Road, a little over one kay apart; her on the high side and me down in the valley.

Bull offers me a lift up there

I remind him I'm nearly eighteen.

'So that'd be a no, would it?'

'See you, Bull – Zoe.' And even though he can't hear me – 'See you, Reggie.'

Trudging up the road I become a part of the landscape, along with the endless sky, the bushland on both sides of me, and the locusts, who never let up on the most boring one-note song in the world.

I've done this walk so many times. Going to see Kayla . . .

We've been friends since we were nine. Back then I wasn't great at conversation. Hello and goodbye were my strong points. Finding something for the middle was always a problem. When the new girl came to school I could see no reason why she'd want to know me.

She had mad legs on her even then, and she's a ranga: long flowing hair the colour of apricots. Dress her in rags, she'd still look hot.

I tried to talk to her a few times, but I think she saw me as a human form of broccoli: she knew I'd probably be good for her, but she didn't like me.

One day it changed.

We were on the school bus, sitting in separate worlds as usual, when she began to sob.

'What's wrong?'

'Buster.' She screwed her eyes up to nothing, but still the tears rolled down. 'My new puppy. He was bitten by a snake. Mum said the vet would save him, but she didn't.'

I got lucky and found the right words to say. There weren't many of them and they weren't important or memorable, but I think they were the right ones. I held onto her hand, too; seemed a natural thing to do, not strange or uncomfortable for either of us. It took a while, but gradually the tears stopped and the smile came out. It was always there, just needed a bit of coaxing.

That day I think we really saw each other for the first time. I mean, saw beyond the bag of bones on the outside. You take away her pretty and my plain and what you get underneath is about the same: a couple of lost girls looking to be found.

As I crest the hill, I see Kayla standing on the road and waving to me. I walk faster.

When we go inside her house she makes a grand announcement to little Harrison.

'Hey. Guess what? Aunty Tiffy's here!'

He looks up for a second. I'm not a cartoon character or a cuddly animal. I'm not an ice-cream or a lolly. All I am is a disappointment.

He goes back to his colouring-in. Smart kid.

I tell Kayla about Reggie.

'He's probably really scared,' she says. 'I feel so sorry for him.'

I'm scared, too. If anything happens to Reggie I don't know how I'll handle it. Don't even want to think about it.

'Where's that nappy monster?'

I could run courses on how to move a conversation in another direction.

'Here she is.' Kayla leads me to the baby's cot. 'Look, Rowie – Aunty Tiffy.'

'Hi, Rowie!' I lean in to give her a kiss, but then instantly lean back out. Something died in there. I've been around the kids lots of times, but I never get used to that smell.

Kayla gets a whiff. 'I think it could be time to change her.'

That just might be the understatement of the year.

'Okay. Let me know when it's done. I'll be outside.'

She grabs my hand. 'Don't even think about making a run for it, Tiff. I know how much you hate changing nappies, but today's the day. Look and learn.'

Kayla peels the dirty nappy from Rowie. The horror! The horror!

'Don't worry about missing out,' she says, 'you'll have a turn before long. Rowie's a machine: food goes in, food comes out; all day, all night.'

There is no way I'm going to have a baby if it leads to this.

At last Rowie is clean and happy, and Harrison is contentedly watching a cartoon. That leaves time for me and Kayla to carry on the way we always do. Our conversation travels down many windy paths, from girls at school who we'd like to see attempt spontaneous combustion, to guys too good to be true, to Kayla's mum's morning sickness, to the odd boy I met at the library, and finally – to wondering if it's possible to be so bored to death you actually die?

Kayla decides it is. 'It's probably like, your heart gets so bored it just goes, "What's the point?" and stops.'

It's fun to rave on like this but we both know there are

important things to talk about. School is over; not just for the year, but forever. We've done Year 12. We're free. That's what we've always wanted, but now that we've got it, it's too big and dark and scary to handle. Summer is nearly at an end and that means life decisions; like heading in different directions, saying, 'I'll see you later', when we don't know how long later might be.

The first major change for me will come on Monday. That's when I start at the *Eagle*. It's officially work experience, but there's a slim hope it could be permanent. Miss Arthur, our English teacher, put in a good word to the editor for me. I don't know what she said, but it was enough for him to give me a chance. The *Eagle* is one of the few papers I know of that still takes on cadets straight out of school. If the editor likes me, if I like the job, if I'm any good at it – if, if, if – I just might get a cadetship.

Kayla has a long, long list of things she *doesn't* want to do with her life. The only thing she's really set her heart on is being an artist. She loves painting – portraits, landscapes, abstracts – anything that involves a brush and colour. At school she was the best at art by far, and she thought that was how it was always going to be. But about two years ago she realised the truth. She's still talented but she's like a six or a seven out of ten, and the world only gives a gold medal to the nines and the tens.

'I'm not worried.' That's what she keeps on telling me.

For now both of us step carefully around the subject of the future. It's one of those too-hard things you leave until you can't put it off any longer. It's much easier to be little kids again, playing show-and-tell.

'Back in a minute.' Kayla jumps up. 'I have to find where Inky put them.'

'Put what?'

'You'll see.'

Kayla's mum has a pretty first name: Bess. But Kayla calls her Inky and her mum doesn't mind, so that's what I call her, too. It's short for 'incubator'. She has a tribe of kids. The one on the way will make six – or is it seven? Let's see . . . there's Rowie and Harrison. Cody and Hales have been fostered and, of course, there's Kayla. Yep, six. There are two or three fathers involved. The latest one is Colin.

He's a lot younger than Inky: good-looking, great body, cheeky smile. She thinks he might be the knight in shining armour that she's always been searching for.

Kayla has her doubts. She keeps on asking me, 'What's a guy like that doing with my mother?'

I understand where she's coming from. Inky's been known to drink too much, she's hooked on pokies, she has a heap of kids, and she's too old for him – other than that they're a perfect match.

I throw out a wild and crazy idea. 'Maybe he really likes her. Maybe he even loves her.'

Kayla groans, but then thinks better of it.

'I shouldn't be such a bitch. You could be right. Mum is a really nice person. He should love her – he better.'

Rowie was only tiny when Inky and Colin met. Rowie's dad had buzzed off and Inky was doing it tough. After not very long at all, Colin was the new man and Inky was pregnant again.

So far he hasn't put a foot wrong. He calls her Bess and says it with affection – I've heard him – and he's got a steady job at the meatworks, he comes home every night, has never once been violent, and doesn't get drunk. What's not to like?

But still Kayla isn't completely persuaded. There's one more major hurdle for him to jump. A new baby's coming. That changes things; lots more pressure. It's the make or break time when guys have to decide if they really want to be a daddy. Rowie's dad fell at that hurdle.

'We'll soon find out how real Colin is,' she says. 'I so hope he doesn't bail.'

'Here you are, just like I promised.'

Kayla drops a large and bulky white envelope onto the table in front of me: her mum's ultrasound pictures.

'You sure she won't mind, Kayla?'

'As if. You're about the only one in Gungee who hasn't

seen them. Inky shows them around like they're happy snaps from a family picnic.'

At first I don't know what to make of what I see. The scans are grey and grainy, shaped like pyramids with a bite taken out of the top of them, or they could be shots of a UFO, or, I know, a dark night sea with just a glint of silver from the moon. But there's not a baby in sight.

'Look there.' Kayla's finger marks the spot.

I make out a vague circle.

'That's Montana,' she says.

'Really? The whole state?'

She ignores my excellent joke. Another witty gem wasted.

'That was a very early one. You keep watching in that same area and see what happens.'

With every new ultrasound the image becomes clearer. I gradually see miniature hands and feet and toes. And then, when I stare really hard, a chubby face appears, looking like one of those Valentine's Day angels.

'Creepy, eh?' says Kayla.

Yep. Creepy and incredible.

'Okay,' she says. 'So, what did you have to show me?'

I reach into my jeans and take out an envelope. Inside is a washed-out photo. My little piece of treasure. I hand it to her without explanation.

She glances at it then back at me, making comparisons. Same eyes, she decides, same mouth.

'This has to be your mother.'

'You got it.'

She studies the photo again.

'Yeah, it's obvious now. You're her. She's you.'

About two months after this photo was taken, I was born and Mum died – clean swap. Caring about someone I never knew doesn't make sense, but that's how it is. This photo means a lot. There must be some invisible mother–daughter wiring that runs from her image in a straight line to my heart.

'My mum's name was Julia.'

She's standing outside a small white house, hands laced together, smiling for the camera.

'And see her huge tummy?'

'It's hard to miss.'

'Well, that's me. Photogenic, aren't I?'

'Yeah, you were at your best then. It's all been downhill since.'

'Thanks, Kayla. You're so full of compliments.'

She takes a closer look at the photo.

'Where'd you get it from?'

'Reggie found it when he was cleaning up some old papers – he doesn't want to leave a mess behind him when he dies.'

'You should tell him to get a life.'

'I do – all the time. Anyway, I think the photo must

have been there ever since I was fostered. It's all I've got of my mum.'

She turns it over to look at the back. It's got names and a date. Even a house number and street.

Forty-one Beamish Street, Surfers Paradise.

As soon as I saw that I copied the address into my journal. Bumped the type size up to twenty-four. Changed the colour to red. All in bold.

'I'm going there one day. Put flowers on Mum's grave. I owe her that.'

'Sounds like a good plan to me.' Kayla nods as if to underline it. 'I know you think about your mum a lot. How about we go there together? Be heaps fun.'

I wanted to ask her but had been afraid she wouldn't be interested. If she'd turned me down, no amount of shrugging would have made it look like I didn't care.

Ever so casually I tell her, 'Hmm. I suppose that would be all right . . . okay, let's do that.'

CHAPTER 9

SOON IT'S TIME FOR Harrison to go back into training – that's potty training. Kayla leaves me in charge while she goes to make a snack, even though I tell her I don't think I ever want to eat again after my experience in nappy hell. She gives me instructions.

'Read a story to him. There's a pile of picture books next to his potty.'

'Doesn't he want privacy?'

She comes back into the room just to fold her arms and stare at me. Okay. I get it.

'Praise him for sitting there. If he does anything, go crazy. If it's a poo, really go mental. You have to clap and he gets a sticker. And for God's sake call me so I can look at it, too.'

'Are you sure I can't make the snack?'

Kayla likes to call this stuff Motherhood Guidance. I think the term she's looking for is Aversion Therapy.

Before long Harrison has some success and I call in Kayla to be a witness, measure and tag it – whatever. And then both of us run around the house like demented chooks – I only copy her, so don't blame me. In later life Harrison will need to see a psychiatrist about this, but for now he thinks we're funny, so mission accomplished. I no sooner step away from him, when Rowie strikes again. And this time it's my turn to change her.

'Yuck!' I hold my hands in front of me and shake them wildly – hoping my fingers might fly off. I have no use for them anymore.

Instead of sympathy, Kayla gives me a high five.

Only two more hours and Inky will be home. She's out with Colin playing pokies at the Royal – and probably flashing the latest set of ultrasounds about.

'All better now,' I say. 'I'm just not used to . . . that.'

'You need more practice.' Kayla bounces Rowie on her knee. That's like stirring a volcano with a stick. 'Should get you doing this more often.'

'Sounds good. I'll put it in the diary for my next free night – that'll be ten years from now, on a Tuesday.'

Kayla isn't really great on amusing comebacks but her eye-rolling is right up there with the very best.

Harrison is on the floor, back at his colouring-in. He looks like he's coping a lot better than me. Little kids are tough. Maybe I'll need to see the shrink before him. I ease into the lounge chair and try to relax.

Kayla picks up Rowie. 'Here's a present for you. I know you've been dying to have a hold.' She plonks the baby onto my lap. 'Don't break her.'

That's exactly what I'm scared of.

'Give her the dummy.

'Don't hold her too tight.

'Or too loose.

'And don't drop her.'

I feel like a blind person, learning to fly.

'Now you've got it. Don't move.'

That's easy. I'm too scared to move.

'Say cheesecake!'

Kayla and her rotten camera phone.

I poke out my tongue as the flash goes off. Rowie giggles and her fingers rake my face.

'She likes you, Tiff.'

I try not to show it, but I'm starting to like her, too. I admit I couldn't see much upside in having a baby at first, but now that she's dry and clean and smelling good, she seems close to perfect.

'You're a natural at this,' Kayla says.

'Sure I am.'

'No, really. You've got all the moves down.'

'What moves? I'm not doing a thing.'

'Yes you are. You're putting out all the right vibes. Babies are like cats. They sense if you like them. She's happy to be with you. Check her out.'

Rowie laughs at that very moment. She does look like she's enjoying herself.

'So how many kids do you think you'll have, Tiff?'

We've been over this ground lots of times; her asking me, me firing it back at her. We have fun with it, but I guess we're also really searching for the answer.

Kayla can never quite decide. One day she doesn't want any kids. Ask her the next day and she wants to have a try at Inky's record. Ask her Sunday morning after a hard night of partying she'll most likely settle for a pet rock.

For me it's a toughy. Any other day, when I haven't got a baby pressed against my chest, I'd know the answer without hesitation. I've thought about guys, sure I have. And I've thought a whole lot about love: how I'd fall right in it one day, and it would be the best fall of my life. But so far I haven't even been in the same country as love – at least not the Heathcliff kind. I think one of the essentials for that to happen is for a guy to actually know I'm alive. I don't get a lot of that.

So I tell myself every chance I get, to help me get used to it –

no guys for me,

no babies

never, ever, ever.

Now I'm not so sure. Somewhere deep down the maternal instinct is stirring, but I know it's going to pass. Has to.

'None.' I hand Rowie back. 'It's just a racket to sell nappies.' I smile as I say it.

'That's my Tiff – not a romantic bone in your body.'

I know Kayla's only joking around but it still cuts into me. I so much want to tell her I didn't mean it, but I don't want to have to explain.

Then she squeezes my hand.

It's like sometimes she knows how my heart feels.

Inky arrives home at ten o'clock. Colin isn't with her.

'Before you go waving your finger, Kayla, no, I didn't have a drink, no, I didn't have a smoke, and no, I didn't lose the family fortune. We set a limit and we kept to it. So give me a kiss and put the kettle on. How are you, Tiff? You two have fun, did you? Kids behave?'

Kayla doesn't move. 'Where's Colin?'

Inky peers all around her, as if expecting to find him.

Then she shrugs.

'Oh dear.' Her face is full of lines that seem to dance when she smiles. 'Looks like I lost another one.'

'Where is he? Did you two have a fight?'

A loud scraping noise comes from outside. Kayla turns on the side light and we both look through the curtain.

Colin's putting out the bins.

'Well how about that?' says Inky. 'I finally got one that's house-trained.'

CHAPTER 10

I HAVE A TERRIBLE NIGHTMARE. And when I wake up I find out that it was true. I'm still here – trapped in Gungee Creek.

Gungee is a very ancient word that means: *this place is a hole.* A very ancient person told me that so it must be right. There just isn't much to do here. Gungee Creek doesn't even have a creek.

There's a cinema complex, of sorts, at Kalatta, but that's two hour's drive away. We'd still claim it as our own if it was a decent size. But, to be honest, it's a slight exaggeration calling it a complex. It's more your inferiority complex cinema, since there's only one, teensy screen.

If you want some hot local entertainment, you can

always head up to Chans and look at the lobsters. They're very playful and happy because no one in Gungee ever orders lobster. They've been there so long I think they're the Chans' family pets. Or if you're not into shellfish you can go to the Royal Arms on a Sunday and watch them draw the meat raffle. Or – yes, there's more – you can sit in Mario's barber shop and listen to his TV. Mario never turns it off and he has it blaring, but there's no picture. It's radio TV. And that just about covers the whole social panorama.

What we do have, though, is football. And we have it today.

It's nine a.m. on Saturday, first game of the pre-season. Already cars jostle for positions around the fence at the oval. Tom Mackenzie, club prezzo, gives the PA a try-out – 'testing, one, two, etcetera, testing' – while small boys in red-and-black footy jerseys pop up on the grass like mushrooms after a rainy day. The Gunners start at under-nines and keep going right through to under-nineties, or thereabouts, which is where Bull fits in.

Every year he makes a solemn announcement: 'This is probably my final season. I'm gettin' too old for this caper.'

I haven't taken much notice before but soon he'll be forty, so maybe he means it this time. The Gunners will find him hard to replace if he retires. Under his captaincy they've notched up about twenty straight losses. It's not every team that can be so consistent. Good one, Bull.

'Look at that big galoot, will yer?'

It's good to hear Reggie's voice – it throbs with life again, not like last night. He points across the road to where Bull runs around the oval in a last-ditch effort to get fit. Reggie opens the window, leans out and roars.

'Oi! Breakfast!'

Bull waves, and plods on.

I have to give Reggie a kiss. Can't help it.

'What was that for?'

'Glad you're okay. That's all. I was really worried about you last night.'

'That was yesterday.' He shrugs. 'Over it now.'

He pours me a cup of tea so strong you could lay bricks on it.

'I googled it,' I say, 'about coughing up blood.'

'Aw, yeah?'

'Seems it's fairly common. You might have burst a tiny blood vessel at the back of your throat.' I don't mind lying for a good cause.

'Really?' He has that look in his eyes like he gets when he backs a winner. 'Probably what it was then. I wasn't too bothered. No dramas.'

'But you should still go and see Anna.' I lean across the table and touch his hand. 'Just so we won't worry. Will you do that? For me?'

'Sounds like blackmail.'

'It is. But you'll do it, won't you?'

'S'pose I'll have to.' He sighs wearily. 'Only way a man's ever gunna get any peace.'

'Thanks, Reggie.'

'Tea strong enough for yer?'

CHAPTER 11

We all set off together for the big game – only have to hike across the paddock. Kayla's here to cheer Bull on, as always. Inky, Colin and the kids will be down soon. Zoe is coming when she finishes her shift at the police station. When the Gunners play, all of Gungee rocks up. If dogs and cats could cheer for the home side, they'd be roped in, too. And Reggie is right in the thick of it. He traipses along beside Bull. Forget that step-dad stuff. It's father and son on days like this.

Reggie started playing for the Gunners when he was a young boy. Now he's the team mascot; their lucky charm. They haven't won a game for ages, but no playing time has been lost due to earthquakes or tsunamis. That has to be a plus. He sits on the team bench with the reserves and the coach, Dusty McTrustry, Gungee's postman. Reggie always wears the team jersey – and a pair of shorts – no matter how cold it gets.

I'm betting he dreams about one day being called on to make a comeback.

'We need five tries in the last three minutes. It's almost impossible, Reggie. That's why I'm asking you.'

'Piece of cake, Dusty. Here, mind me false teeth.'

Dusty's been with the Gunners as long as I can remember. He's an institution – or he should be in one – it's one of the two. The boys aren't really into training so his main job through the season is to tell jokes and cheer everyone up. He's like a grief counsellor for bad footballers.

Kayla and I spread our blanket out on the Grandstand, a long grassy mound looking down over the oval. We can see the whole town trooping in from here. There's Mrs Muir. She stands out because of her pink umbrella. Further along are Joel and Dominique, holding hands and swinging their arms like kids.

There are people I'm always glad to see, like my old primary school teacher, Mrs Smiffy. It took me a few years to realise her real name is Smith, but I still kept calling her Smiffy – same as everyone else. And here comes Gabe and his new girlfriend, Amelia. Hope she likes living with his mum.

Now I see Inky with Rowie in a baby stroller. And Colin. He lifts Harrison off his shoulders, plants him lightly on the ground and chases him, making monster noises as Harrison squeals. Colin catches me looking at him and smiles, open and friendly. I swing from his face to Inky's; line them up and compare. He has a wild and handsome look – think of some swashbuckling movie pirate. She looks like a tuck-shop mum, her face permanently creased with tiredness from years of being on-call for crying babies. It crosses my mind that Inky won't keep him for long.

Hey! Be positive! I tell my mind.

Scattered applause breaks out as the ref and the linesmen jog onto the field. We hold up our banner when Bull lumbers past with his teammates.

'GO THE GUNS!'

Kayla puts two fingers between her teeth and does her famous whistle – better than any boy – while I stand up to applaud.

Bull spots us and gives his two-thumbs salute, trotting backwards. Imm-pressive! All those years of practice are starting to pay off – his footy is still woeful but he's got the reverse trot down to a fine art.

The Tarwyn Blues are just like the Gunners. They don't have enough players in the local derby to fit them all perfectly into their respective age brackets. If you're ugly enough and big enough to play with the middle-aged baldies, you're in. So I'm not all that surprised when I see Big Foot jog onto the field.

'Let's pay him back,' says Kayla when I point him out. 'Every time he gets tackled, we cheer. If he drops the ball, we cheer even louder. But I don't think we should boo. We don't want to be bad sports. Do we?' She crinkles up her nose as she thinks it through. 'Aw what the hell – let's boo him.'

'No. We won't do any of that stuff. We are going to ignore him.'

'But it'll be fun, Tiff. And he deserves it.'

'You don't get it, Kayla. I don't want him to know I'm here. Please, let's just sit here quietly. Okay?'

'I'll do my best,' she says.

CHAPTER 12

'BULL'S GOT THE BALL!

'Yes!

'He's running hard!

'Watch out!

'He steps through the tackle!

'Goooo, Bullll!

'He dodges, weaves and – *ouch* – nasty.'

Apparently, this is Kayla's best. Great!

Again and again I ask her to keep it down. I don't need the commentary, but she's determined I'm not going to miss a thing. Why? I'm only here to support Bull and the team, and try to lift their spirits after they've lost. Until then I'm quite content to sit out the duration of the massacre, buried deep in the French Revolution, thanks to a little red pocket edition of *A Tale of Two Cities* that I bought at a garage sale for fifty cents. It's the perfect companion for buses, trains, and football games where I'm trying to be invisible.

'Tiff! Tiff!'

'She's not here.'

'Look, look!'

I humour her, hoping to see Bull doing something spectacular, but it's only his bum she's going on about. His head's in the scrum and a goodly portion of his pale and pimpled behind is sticking out, his shorts and underdaks at half-mast. Kayla thinks it's hilarious; too much information for me.

Since I've already been distracted, I take a quick peek at Big Foot. He looks awfully confused. I don't think he's had much practice at this game. Now he's got his arms folded. Now he's scratching himself. Now he breaks into a half-hearted trot. He runs as if he's borrowed someone else's legs for the day and they're not his size. It isn't a good look. But at least he runs in the right direction – most of the time.

Where was I? Ah, yes . . .

'Every day, through the stony streets, the tumbrels now jolted heavily, filled with Condemned.'

'Tiff.' Kayla nudges my book. 'Your guy isn't much of a player.'

'You know what this is about?' I show her the cover.

'Of course.'

'Then you know I'm too worried about the guillotine to care about football – and by the way, he's not my guy.'

'Glad to hear it. He is hopeless out there.'

'I don't think he's all that bad.' I always go for the underdog. 'At least he's made two tackles.'

'You call them tackles?' Kayla gives me her astounded gape. 'He lost his balance when he was doing up his shoelaces, that's what they were.'

'Get ready to take that back.'

I stand for a better view as Big Foot leaps high to take a pass. Now he's worked out how to use his legs and the line's wide open. And he's charging.

Kayla jumps up. 'Stop him! Stop him!'

Only one person can reach him before he scores.

Bull.

Everyone at the ground is on their feet and roaring. Gungee Creek hasn't seen such excitement since they put in the flashing forty kay lights outside the primary school.

As if he's trying to fly, Bull launches himself through the air, actually flies for one glorious second, and then comes crashing ingloriously down. Big Foot evades him easily and crosses over for three points while Bull is still skidding across Gungee Oval. He really needs to wear a parachute if he plans to do any more tackling.

This one mighty try unlocks the avalanche and the Blues go on a scoring rampage. For all of five minutes the

Gunners fight back valiantly but then reality sets in. If you could put subtitles to their body language it would say: 'Ah, stuff it. This is too much like hard work.'

CHAPTER 13

By half-time the local lads are done for. The guy with the ice-cream van is doing a fair trade, but if he sold black armbands he'd make a fortune.

'I think we should get a girls' team together next year,' Kayla says. 'We'd have to be better than these losers.'

The Blues prance off the oval like cup-winning race-horses: straight backs and beaming smiles. The Gunners limp and trudge, heads down and shoulders sagging. A crane couldn't lift their morale, though Dusty tries his best.

'"A" for effort, men,' he says as they straggle past. 'Don't worry about the score – numbers mean nothing – you'll run over the top of them in the second half.'

There's no clubhouse at Gungee. The teams change in

the toilets and flop down on the grass at the break. Both sides are only four or five metres away from us.

Dusty picks his way over a battlefield of bloodied arms and legs, dispensing oranges, bandaids and fatherly slaps on the back. He doesn't bother with a motivational speech. The boys need their rest.

I look around for Big Foot and see him at the same time as he sees me.

'Hiiii!'

I act as if I don't hear him.

'Hiiii!'

It's like pretending you don't hear a foghorn when it's stuck in your ear.

I give him the smallest wave I've got. That's all the encouragement he needs. He bounds up to me, smiling broadly.

'Hey. Library girl. Thought it was you.'

'Hey. Toilet boy.'

'Toilet boy – good one. How's it goin'?'

'It's going really good.' I show him my book. 'I'm up to a very exciting part and I just can't wait to find out what happens.'

That's about as big a hint as I can give, but hints only work if the other person is listening.

'Got a bit lucky out there,' he says. 'Scored a try. This is only my second game, too. You see it?'

'No. When?'

'Just then. In the game.'

'Oh. Interesting. Shame I missed it. I was reading.' I turn to Kayla. 'Did you see anything?'

'Nuh. Not me. What happened?'

'Yeah, sure.' He smiles. 'Almost had me goin' there. I'm Davey.'

'I'm Kayla.'

As they shake hands he says, 'Well, that's two people I know in Gungee Creek: Kayla and my pal from the library – Tiffany.'

He remembered.

'You don't mind if I call you that, do you? I really like that name.'

'She hates it,' Kayla says. 'Don't you, Tiff?'

'Um . . . sometimes I don't mind it.'

'Come on!' bellows one of his team mates. 'We're waitin' for yer!'

'One minute!' He turns back to us. 'The coach wants to give us some pointers. He's all into motivation and–'

I tune out from what he's saying and tune in to looking at him. The negatives are hard to ignore. He's a Big Foot all right, with a dash of Neanderthal thrown in. His body is ungainly and sprawling; hard to know where the muscles end and the fat takes over. And his bushy hair, which can't make up its mind if it's black or brown, sticks out at all angles and is streaked with grass stains, dirt and a liberal drenching of sweat.

There's not a whole lot on the plus side, unless you're a soppy idiot who believes in stuff like kindness. I can't help feeling he's got that. It's in his voice, his smile and his eyes.

'Numbnuts!'

Big Foot blushes. 'They call everyone that.'

'Over here. Move it!'

'Gotta go! See yers!'

And he runs.

Kayla watches me, watching him.

'You like him, don't you, Tiff?'

'Puleeze. Give me more credit than that.'

'Okay then. What's so wrong with him?'

'He's not my type.'

'What is your type?'

'Normal.'

CHAPTER 14

TOM MACKENZIE'S VOICE BOOMS over the loudspeaker.

'We've got a couple of raffles to draw today: one for Gungee, one for Tarwyn. Have your tickets ready.'

It's the perfect excuse to escape from Kayla before she asks any more dumb questions. Mrs Muir is straining to read the numbers on her tickets, and I'm glad to help out.

'No, you haven't got that one. Or that one. Or that one. Sorry, Mrs Muir. That's all there is. You didn't win.'

'That's quite all right, dear.' She gives me a smile like a sunflower. 'I have a lovely time just being alive. A person can't be too greedy.'

I like Mrs Muir. She always cheers me up.

On the way back to Kayla I stop off to see Reggie. He says he's feeling awful.

'Stay right there and I'll get Bull,' I tell him. 'We'll take you home.'

'Why? There's nothin' wrong with me. It's the Guns. They're gettin' hammered. That's why I feel awful.'

'Dusty oughta get you out there,' I say. 'You'd soon turn things around.'

'Couldn't do any worse, luv.'

Next stop is Bull.

'You are playing a complete blinder.' I lower my voice. 'But your back must be aching. You're carrying the whole team.'

'True, mate,' Bull says. 'Bloody hopeless lot they are. Only trouble is I taught 'em everything they know.'

A strong hand grips my shoulder. I look up and see Zoe.

'Hi ya, Tiff.' Bull gets a kiss. 'Sorry I'm late. What's the story? Are we winning?'

I leave it for him to break the bad news.

'Catch you later.'

Then I'm back with Kayla for The Slaughter, Part Two. It's not a lot of fun to watch the pride of Gungee getting squashed under foot. Of all the team's supporters I'm the only one who has a moderately good time. Thanks heaps, Mr Dickens.

Now and again I look up to see how Big Foot is doing.

It's purely zoological curiosity. He's a strange beast; unlike the boys I know. Or maybe I only think that because he's cheerful and friendly – and when he talked to me just now there wasn't a raffle book in sight. I'm sure he's not interested in me, not really, though it's comforting to know that there are guys like him out there – weird, gangling, goofball guys. But nice ones.

With fifteen minutes in the game still to go, the loyal Gunners' fans start packing up and searching for their car keys. I understand how they feel. It's forgivable to drive slowly past the scene of a disaster, but after nearly two hours and a picnic lunch you really should leave.

'Oopsy.'

Clash of heads in a tackle. Big Foot and Bull. It looked like an accident but that doesn't matter. I've seen this sort of thing before and I know where it's going.

Big Foot pushes Bull, who shoves back just as hard.

I can't look.

Have to look.

Please don't hurt him, Bull.

They spar around for a few seconds and then Big Foot starts throwing punches. Bull blocks one with his mouth but isn't fazed. He raises his fists and crouches low, dancing about and looking dangerous. It's like a warning: 'This is what I've got. I was a boxer. I can take you anytime. Don't mess with me.'

Big Foot punches him again. Another mouth block. Suddenly it swings from boxing to wrestling as Bull goes for the body slam, sending him sprawling backwards. Now both of them are rolling on the ground and trying to kill each other.

Their teammates pull them apart just as the ref marches up. He points to the sidelines and shouts, 'Off! Both of you! Off!'

They slouch from the field together. Bull's buddies give him a cheer and a 'Good on you' and he responds with a cheesy grin. No one boos or hurls abuse at Big Foot – either because we're a friendly bunch or he's simply too damn big to mess with. Just the same, he keeps his head down all the way; looks to be taking it bad. The Blues' support team waits for him as he goes through the gate. He pushes past them, refusing to talk or listen. His mouth is bloodied and that look on his face is familiar. He's stolen it from me: it's my furious, 'I hate the world' look. But it's a lot worse than mine ever was.

My eyes follow him as he runs up the hill, pulls open the door of the team bus, climbs in and slumps into a window seat. For a moment he looks at me. Or did I imagine it? Then he ducks his head down and he's gone.

Of course, my loyalty is to Bull, but a quick glance tells me he's in good hands. He's got a few minor cuts and scrapes, that's all. Reggie is on one side of him and on the other is Zoe. He's being fussed over and he's lapping it up. Doesn't need me.

Kayla says something – Where you going? What are you doing? – one of those. I'm not even sure if I answer. All my attention turns to Big Foot.

I follow the path he took up the hill, and knock on the door of the bus.

Nothing.

'Just tell me you're okay. That's all I want to know.'

Nothing.

'Then I'll have to smash a window – because you might be hurt, you might be bleeding to death. If you don't talk to me I have no way of knowing. So stay right there while I go find a brick . . .'

I back my judgement and don't go anywhere. In only a couple of seconds the door swings open and I step up and go inside.

Big Foot slumps behind the driver's seat, head buried in his hands.

'Thanks for letting me in.'

'Sawright.'

'I've got a bad temper, too.'

He sighs. It's like he's saying: 'When is she going to leave me alone?' When I'm good and ready – that's when.

'Sometimes I just lose it' – I'm thinking of The Great Sunflower Attack – 'but usually I'm able to control myself because I've developed an anger management technique. You want to hear about it?'

'Not really.'

'Well, what it is, see, is I drop books on people I'm angry with.'

'Look, Tiffany–'

The more I hear him say my name, the more I like it.

'I don't feel like talking right now. Maybe some other time.'

'Sure, sure. I get it. That's exactly how I am when I'm angry. Bull comes to talk to me – he's the one you punched, by the way. He's like my uncle, big brother – take your pick – it's complicated. He's also a cop. Of all the guys out there, you pick the cop to punch. Good one. Anyway, Bull comes into my room and I go mental and throw stuff at him and tell him to rack off – only I don't say rack. But, you know, I really like it that he makes the effort. That's why I thought I'd come over and see you. Didn't want you to be angry all on your own.'

He looks up at me. At last.

'You're a weird chick, aren't you?' That's what he says to me.

'Good observation.' That's what I answer.

A glad, happy look breaks out on his face. I mean, really breaks out, as if it's been held captive by the forces of doom and gloom and now it's on his face and stretching out and smiling at me.

'So you drop books on people?'

'Yep.'

'And that's a good thing?'

'Aw yeahh. Not real books because I would never damage a book. No way. What I do is – say I'm you. Right?'

'You're me.'

'Okay. I'm playing footy. Having a fine time. And then this gorilla headbutts me. I realise later it was an accident, but at the time I'm not in a fit state to realise anything, because all I can think of is killing the fool. You with me so far?'

'I might even be ahead of you.'

'Good. Now here's where our approach differs. Instead of punching out like a maniac, as you did, I would have closed my eyes and used my imagination to build a plane.'

He looks doubtful. Can't imagine why.

'Trust me. This works. I do it all the time and I can't even use a screwdriver. I build the plane – it takes a second – jump in and take off. Then I swoop low over the head of my victim and wave at him from the cockpit. That alone feels amazing. He starts running and I can see the fear on his face, but there's nowhere to hide. Now here comes the really good part. I open the bomb doors. One thousand copies of *War and Peace* land on him –

'Five hundred and sixty thousand words in each book.

'Hard back covers.

'Large print edition.

'The pen is mightier than the sword!'

He mulls it over for a second, before telling me what he thinks.

'Yeah,' he says, nodding, 'you are full-on weird.' But he says it with a smile.

It seems like a perfect time to leave – while I'm winning.

When I get back to Kayla she's full of questions for me. I give her answers trimmed to the bone.

'Just thought I'd make sure he was all right.

'He hardly said anything.

'I said a lot of rubbish.

'And no, I don't expect to ever see him again.'

That night I type the day's adventures into my journal. For the first time I don't call him Big Foot. He's Davey.

CHAPTER 15

ON SUNDAY THEY HAVE an eight-dollar dinner special at the Royal. Kayla and I never miss it. I go for the shepherd's pie with chips and she has the lasagna with chips. If you eat at the Royal, you'd better like chips.

We find an empty table in a corner, but before long it's noisy. Meat raffle's on. Charlie Dent is in charge. He's quite a poet. Especially when he works with colours.

'Twenty-nine blue – could that be you?'

'Thirty-three green – has anyone seen – thirty-three green?'

And he's known far and wide for this one:

'Fifty-six pink – rinky-dink-dink!'

It's so bad it's funny. But Kayla isn't laughing tonight. She isn't all that bothered about food either. Not long into the meal she abandons her knife and fork to graze on the chips, seeking out the slightly burnt crispy ones. But she soon tires of that.

'Can we get outta here, Tiff?'

That's fine with me. We both know a quieter place. It's a fair trek but it's on our way home and there's a short cut. In fifteen minutes we're standing at the entrance to our own private hide-out: Gungee Creek Cemetery.

I lead the way. There's one floodlight near the street but the further in among the graves we go, the more the darkness buries us.

Hot nights bring out snakes so I warn Kayla to be careful.

Immediately she shrieks, 'Tiff! Tiff! Behind you!'

It's a feeble old joke and only an idiot would fall for it.

She cackles when I jump.

As we usually do, we prop ourselves up against the headstones of Monnie and Grogan Nash. Being buried together means they have a double-sized slab of concrete in front of them, which is perfect for us to sit on. We don't mean any disrespect. It's just that they feel like old friends and I know they'd want us to be comfy. They've both been dead for over a hundred years, but we still say hello to them. However, we don't ask how they are. That would be tactless.

From out of her backpack Kayla produces a Coke bottle.

The drink's all gone and now it's half-filled with a clear liquid.

'Vodka. Nicked it from Inky. If she misses it, which I doubt, she won't mind.' She dives back into her bag. 'Got a couple of paper cups in here, too, somewhere, ah, here we go.'

We've been coming here for years; had a few beers on burning hot days, but we've never drunk vodka before.

'So what's the deal?' I ask.

'You start at the paper tomorrow. That's special.'

'Only work experience.'

'But you might get a cadetship – that's what you said – right?'

'A long shot.'

'You'll get it.'

She brushes her cup against mine. 'Cheers! But don't scull it – that is deadly stuff.'

I take a sip, and grimace. 'It's horrible.'

'Give it a chance to grow on you.'

'I've got enough things growing on me already, thanks.'

'Drink.'

I have another gulp and roll it around my mouth. It still burns my lips, my tongue.

'Better?'

It's the closest I've ever come to drinking diesel, but I don't want to spoil her fun.

'Getting there.'

She doesn't see me tip it out.

A yawn is followed by a stretch, and then, as if she's in her own bed instead of on top of a gravestone, Kayla lies on her side, hands cupped under her cheek to make a pillow.

'This wouldn't be such a bad place to end up.' A sliver of moon shines enough light for me to see that her eyes are closed; it's almost like she's talking in her sleep. 'You'd be right at home here, Tiff. Nice and peaceful, like the library. Throw a few books in with you and you'd be happy.'

'The dead can't read.'

'You don't know that for sure. They could have reading clubs, right here in Gungee Cemetery. Now there's something for you to look forward to.'

'Go to sleep, Kayla. I'll wake you up if anyone wants to read you a story.'

She's quiet for a couple of minutes but awake, and restless . . .

'Knock, Knock,' she says. 'Anyone home?'

'No.'

'I've been thinking about things lately . . .'

A slight tension grips at me; I don't quite know why, except that Kayla sounds very serious. I'm not used to that.

'What kind of things?'

'Well . . . do you think I'll ever get a job?'

'Of course, you idiot, I know you will.'

'I've got the same genes as Inky and she's never had one.'

'But she's got kids. That's her job.'

'Yeah, great. Thanks for reminding me.' She sits up now, perched on the edge of the grave. 'It'll probably be mine too. I'm getting just like her. I drink and I smoke–'

'Thought you quit.'

'That was last week.'

'Oh.'

'And in about five years from now I'll have two or three little snots and they'll make up some crappy nickname for me, like Inky, and I'll still be here in Gungee.'

'How much of that vodka have you had?'

'Not enough.'

'Well you're mad. You don't have to stay here. You can leave anytime you want.'

'I've got no cash, no car, and my mum is pregnant and she needs me – she always needs me. You tell me how I'm–'

'Stop. Just stop, Kayla. Things will change. Life is going to work out fine.'

'How can you say that? You don't know what's gunna happen.'

'Sure I do. I'll become rich and famous and I won't forget you.'

'Thanks.'

'No problem. I'll hire you as my maid.'

'That's right – make a joke of it. You think everything's a joke, Tiff, but it's not.'

'Huh? I was only trying to lighten things up.'

'Yeah, I know – and I gotta tell ya, it is so annoying when you do that. I don't need you to lighten up what I say – I need you to understand!'

'Okay, okay. I understand!'

'No! You don't!'

'Fine! Whatever you say, Kayla.'

The silence batters us. It builds to a crescendo. She breaks first.

'Damn you, Tiff. Now look what you've done.'

'Me? What did I do?'

'You've made me feel guilty for being so mean . . . I'm sorry.'

'You were just being honest.'

'No I wasn't. I was being jealous.'

'No way! Of me?'

'Yes, you. Your job . . . and now I feel awful, because I know you'd never be jealous of me.'

'Don't be so sure.'

'Oh, I'm sure all right. You never get jealous.'

'Wrong, Kayla. Dead wrong. I just never show it.'

'You're kidding me, right?'

'No. I'm dead serious. Everyone likes you, Kayla. You fit in anywhere you go. You can eat anything you like and not put on weight – which isn't fair, but you can't help it – and you're pretty and generous and–'

'Are you trying to make me throw up?'

'All I've got is a smart mouth.'

'That's not true.'

'And like you say, that gets very annoying. I don't know why you have anything to do with me.'

'Good point. I don't know either. Why should I bother with someone who says such absolute garbage?'

'It's true about you not putting on any weight . . .'

'Okay. From now on I'm stocking up on chocolates and ice-creams. Watch this space. Skinny me is gone!'

'I don't want you to do that. You can be skinny. No one's perfect.'

'Hey.' Her pinky finger nudges mine. 'I love your smart mouth. I don't want you to change anything.'

I lean back against the cold stone and gaze around me. In among the dead there must be girls who were once like me and Kayla. They probably lived this very scene before us; asked the same questions about friendship, about life; wondered if it was all worthwhile. I think it is. Hope it is.

CHAPTER 16

ON SATURDAY, WHILE HE had the Gunners for company, Reggie forgot about being sick and old. I took a ton of photos of him at the barbecue after the game: in his short shorts with his toothpick legs; tackling a giant beer like an ambitious sparrow; telling anyone who would listen what they did wrong and how he would have done it so much better. No one got upset with him. Reggie's a legend, that's what they all said. I don't think he wanted that day to ever end.

But now it's Monday. He's dressed up in his brown suit coat and pants and shiny black shoes. Wearing his natty felt hat, too – the one with the yellow feather stuck in the brim. He wants that with him when he's cremated.

All this for his appointment to see Anna.

'She's only a doctor,' Bull reminds him. 'Not the bloody Queen.'

'Come from the old school, I do,' Reggie says, 'where we had respect. A man doesn't want to look like a no-hoper.'

I ask him where his tie is, just for a stir, because I know what the answer will be.

'Don't believe in 'em,' he says. 'You can get in all kinds of strife with ties. Oh yes. My very word.'

I've heard his killer-tie stories many times.

It just doesn't make any sense puttin' a noose around your own neck. You put it on too tight and you half choke to death; too loose and its liable to fly up and get caught in a train door. And then there's–

But today I don't ask him to explain the dangers. I'd like to have a laugh – just to myself – but I've got somewhere I have to be.

The bus to Menindah takes an hour. I've left myself plenty of time to make it to the *Eagle* by nine.

Bull has other ideas.

'I have to call in at the courthouse there this morning,' he says. 'You might as well keep me company on the drive.'

'Forget it. I'm not going with you in the cop car.'

'Won't kill yer.' He checks out the mirror as he goes past. Looks disappointed at what he finds there. 'You ready?'

'Everyone will think I'm under arrest.'

'Especially when I put the cuffs on yer.'

'You're an idiot, Bull.'

'So I've been told, but who cares what anyone thinks? Don't worry about it. You can get the bus for the rest of the week.'

'But–'

'No buts. It's a done deal. We can drop off Reggie as we go through town.'

Reggie bristles at this. 'Nah. I'll be right. Got me walkin' shoes on.'

'Forget that. Anna's expecting you there sometime this week.'

'Eughhh.'

In fifteen minutes we pull up in front of Anna's surgery. Bull gives Reggie a card with the cop shop's number on it.

'Someone should be there. Give them a bell when you're ready. They'll organise a lift home – don't try to walk it. Don't want you dropping dead on the side of the road. This is a tidy town, yer know.'

Reggie pokes his head through the window.

'See what I gotta put up with, Tiffy? Talk about flamin' police brutality.'

'Haven't started on you yet.' Bull winks at me. 'You go ahead and walk home, old bloke – I've been looking for an excuse to try out the taser.'

'Yeah, yeah.' Reggie slaps the car door. 'See yer, Tiffy.'

We drive off quickly. I turn around, watching Reggie as long as I can. He looks unsteady on his feet.

Tell me again he's going to be okay, Bull. I say it to myself, but somehow he hears it.

'Stop worryin', mate.' His gnarly fist scrapes against my jaw. 'Anna'll fix him up.'

The towns whiz by. Bull eyes the clock on the dash. 'Should make it right on time. You must be chuffed about this. Finally gettin' a start at a paper. How's it feel?'

'All right.'

'Can't you do better than that? You have to be excited. You wanted to be a reporter from way back – used to cut stories out of the paper when you were a little girl. Then you'd rearrange them and stick them in a book – made your own newspapers. Remember that?'

'Not me. I'd never do anything that lame.'

'You gotta stop trying to be cool, Tiff. Doesn't do a thing for me.'

That's because you don't know what cool is, Bull! You've never had a cool day in your life! In fact, the only thing cool about you, is me! I almost say those things, but then I remember he's got a gun.

'This is your dream job,' he says. 'You've always told me that. Right or wrong?'

'I suppose.'

'You're on a roll. Don't stop. Now tell me what you're really feeling.'

'Well . . . I guess I am a little bit excited.'

'Good.'

'And scared – because it's all new and I don't know what I'm going to have to do or what the people will be like . . . but I think it's a good scared.'

Bull smiles. It's like he's just dragged a confession out of a suspect.

We're behind a line of cars at a traffic light when we hear a siren. I see a fire-truck across the road on our left. Cars pull over to let it pass and it sneaks through the lights and speeds off.

'Do you think we should follow it?' I ask.

'Why would we want to do that?'

'In case it's a big story. I could write an eyewitness report.'

'You've seen too many movies.'

'I'm serious, Bull. The editor said he wanted someone who showed initiative. There's not going to be a better chance than this.'

'But he's going the opposite way to us. If we chase after him there's a good chance you'll be late for your job.'

'No guts, no story. Please follow him.'

He turns off the highway, mumbling to himself. And

soon we're on the same road as the fire-truck, but way behind.

'Can you go faster? I can only just see him. We won't be able to hear his siren in a minute.'

'There's a speed limit.'

'You're a cop, Bull. *Hello.*'

He grits his teeth and plants his foot down on the accelerator.

'Happy now?'

'That's much better. What about the siren?'

'No. No. Positively no.'

'Just a short burst to get those cars out of the way – we're gunna lose him if you don't. One tiny little–'

'Bloody hell! This is the last time I give you a lift anywhere!'

Bull hits the siren. Cars slow and shift across lanes to let us through. We soon catch up to the fire-engine guy, who surprises us when he switches off his siren, moves to the side of the road, and stops.

'Oh, jeez.' Bull covers his face with his hands. 'He probably thinks I was trying to pull him over.'

'I'll go and explain it to him,' I say.

'No you will not. Stay here – I'll do it.'

He's about to get out of the car but changes his mind when the firey hops down from the truck and hurries back to us.

'Everything all right, officer? No problem, is there?'

Bull leans out the window. 'No. You're right, mate. You just keep on your way. Thought I'd follow you to the fire, that's all – case I can lend a hand.'

'Oh, I see. Right. Yeah . . .'

This guy is sweating bullets. Nervous as. Even Bull picks up on it.

'Anything wrong, buddy?' he asks.

'Well, um – to tell you the truth, I wasn't actually going to a fire. It was more like a drill.'

'A drill, eh?'

Bull gives me a knowing glance – like he's saying, 'we're on to somethin' here' – and gets out of the car.

'Think I might wander over and have a gander at your truck, mate.' He's already on his way, the driver trying to keep up. 'You got some ID I can have a look at?'

Suddenly the fire-engine's siren begins wailing.

The firey yells, 'Rory! No! No! Turn it off!'

A kid of about six or seven sticks his head out of the window and waves gleefully to us from the fire-truck before the siren is switched off.

'Sorry, officer.' The guy's in his sixties but that doesn't stop his face from lighting up as red as the fire-engine. 'I'm minding the grandson this morning.' He shows Bull his ID. 'You know how kids are – he wanted to hear the siren. I was only going to take him around the block.'

Bull puts on his stern-copper face. 'Yeah, well, it's not real good, is it? A man in your position should know better.'

'I know. I'm sorry.'

'You can't just use community property to take your grandkid on a joyride.'

'It won't happen again, officer. I promise.'

Bull folds his arms. Sighs. Glares. And then finally . . .

'All right. I'm going to let it go this once.'

'Aw, thanks, mate – officer. That's really decent of you.'

'But if I hear any reports about you doin' this again–'

'You won't. I swear.'

'Go on. Get back to work then – and leave the kid with someone else next time.'

The poor firey is still muttering 'thank you' as we drive away. I can only manage to wait ten seconds before I laugh.

'Bull, you are such a hypocrite.'

'Yeah,' he says, 'but it was fun.'

Because of the fire-engine detour I don't make it to the *Eagle* till quarter past nine. Bull offers to go in with me and say it's his fault I'm late. I know it's a nice gesture, but I have to pass. Can't take the risk of him saying something dumb or tripping over the furniture or accidentally shooting the editor.

'You're not embarrassed about me, are you?' he asks.

'Of course not.'

Just drive away real fast so they don't see I've turned up in a cop car.

CHAPTER 17

'SORRY I'M LATE.'

The editor's name is Andrew Matthews. He's a big unit, same scale as Bull, except that he's got a belly you could sit a vase of flowers on. And he's maybe ten years older, and bald, and his glasses are way big and behind them are small green eyes that are staring at me.

'Late on your first day? That's not a very promising start.'

His feet are up on the desk and his hands are behind his head as he slowly rocks back and forth. I wasn't going to mention the fire-engine because it didn't quite work out the way I'd hoped, but he looks at me as though he'd be disappointed if he didn't get an excuse.

'There was a fire-engine, Mr Matthews. That's why I'm a fraction late.'

'Oh, I see. And why would that make you late?'

'Well, it went past us and the siren was going, so I decided to follow it in case there was a major fire. When we talked on the phone you said to show some initiative.'

'Ah. And was there a fire?'

'Um, I don't think so, no, not quite.'

'Oh well. Never mind – tomorrow's another day.'

I'm not quite sure what he means by that but I have a feeling sarcasm might be involved. Pressing on, I hand him a folder.

'There's a few references there.' One's from Bull – don't know if that's allowed or not seeing as he's hardly impartial. 'And a copy of my Year 12 results.'

He drops the folder on the desk without looking at it.

'Good.' He lifts his feet off the desk and stands up. 'Now we better get you organised. You would have met Nancy when you came in?'

'Yep.'

'Anything you want to know, Nancy's the one.' He opens the door and ushers me out. 'I'll be around today but after that you won't see much of me. Head office has me booked in at an editors' seminar most of the week. But you'll be working with a very experienced journalist. One of the best.'

He calls out to the only person in sight.

'Shark.'

A lanky, silver-haired guy glances up from his computer. I'm betting he slept in his clothes. Needs a shave and a haircut and a good soak in the fountain of youth. Looks like an unloved antique.

'That'd be me. What can I do you for?'

'Got a new starter for you.' The editor pats me on the shoulder – or is it a push out the door? 'Off you go, girl. Oh, and by the way, the name's Andrew – not Mr Matthews.'

I want to tell him my name's not 'girl', it's Tiff. Not brave enough.

The antique stands up, waiting for me like a gentleman.

'Hi, I'm–' That's as far as I get.

'You'd have to be work experience, wouldn't you?'

I admit that I am – I can tell he's not too thrilled about it – but I still blather on about maybe getting a cadetship, if–

That's as far as I get. Again.

'This'll be your computer. Ever used a computer before?'

'Sure.'

'I don't mean for playing games – Facebook or Twitter or any of that stuff. You ever used a computer for writing?'

'All the time. I write short stories and poetry, and I've tried doing a novel but it hasn't worked out yet. I'm thinking I might write a play.'

'That so?'

'Yep.'

'Well, good for you. But you can forget about all that now. It's crap. Did you see the sign out the front? This is the *Eagle*. It's a newspaper. What we do is news. No fairies. No vampires. No goblins. Meat-and-potato news. How's that grab yer?'

'Um . . . good.'

He thrusts a hand at me. 'They call me The Shark. You know why?'

'No.'

'Because when I sniff blood – I go for it. I circle a story and I wait. Then I strike. They call me The Shark.'

'They call me Tiff.'

The Shark grunts as we shake hands.

'I can teach you everything there is to know about newspapers; been at this game forty years. But let's cut to the chase – get the most important thing out of the way first.' He hands me a grotty, brown-stained cup. 'I take my tea strong; milk, no sugar. Kitchen's out the back. You'll find the urn is boiling right now.'

My first thought is to tell him to go jump in the urn – Bull and Reggie would never treat me like this – but instantly I suppress that impulse. He's my boss and I'm a work-experience girl – the lowest of the low. I get the feeling I'm going to be seeing a lot of the kitchen.

'Okay . . . Shark.'

At the urn I run into Nancy again. We talked briefly when I first got here.

'I see Richard already has you making his tea for him. He doesn't waste any time.'

'Is Richard the same as the Shark?'

'Oh yes. Richard Park, that's his real name. Poor old Shark. I think he made that name up himself. We humour him. Takes himself far too seriously, that man. Between you and me I think he's more like a goldfish than a shark. If he called himself Guppy I could see the sense in it.'

Once I've delivered the Shark's tea – in a freshly washed cup, which he doesn't notice – Nancy 'borrows' me for a minute so I can meet the rest of the staff. There are only three of them. Two are ad reps: Sue and Warren. They're both on the phone so I only get a nod, but that's okay as I'm told I won't be having much to do with them. They're in a separate part of the office to us.

'But you will be seeing a lot of my good friend here,' Nancy says.

Jordie, the photographer: smouldering blue eyes, thick shoulder-length black hair.

'My kids go to kinder with his,' Nancy adds. 'His wife, Emma, teaches there. Lovely family.'

I don't really like smouldering blue eyes that much anyway.

'Great to know you.' He half whispers, like he's telling me a secret. 'Now stand just over here.' He positions me against a door. 'And let me see a smile.'

One wall of the kitchen is covered with photos.

'That's the rogues' gallery,' Nancy explains. 'Every person who's ever worked at the *Eagle* is up there.'

I hate having my photo taken but before I can wriggle out of it, Jordie points his camera and clicks.

'You'll be there with the rest of the troops by this afternoon, Tiff.' He gives me a thumbs-up. 'Welcome to the *Eagle*.'

By nine-forty I'm back at my desk and ready to work. The Shark is hard at it, punching out stories so fast it's a wonder the computer isn't smoking. I log on, type in the password I've been given, and wait to be told what to do next. No one tells me a thing.

At ten-forty the Shark goes to the loo. A thesaurus on the desk catches my attention. Inside the cover it says: *To: Richard Park. From: Richard Park.* He gives a book to himself and writes an inscription, like it's a present? That is sad. I delve further inside and on the very first page I come to, there's a squashed cockroach. It's long dead but its antenna sticks up in the air like it's waving at me. Gross!

I dump the book and pounce on the Shark when he comes back.

'Is there anything I can do to help?'

'What you're doing is brilliant. Winning formula. Don't change a thing.'

'But I'm not doing–'

'Sweetheart, I got a crook hip and today it's giving me all kinds of curry. But I haven't got time to feel sorry for myself because I've got a paper to put out. Stopping to hold your hand just isn't on. We'll sit down and have a cosy chat tomorrow, when it isn't deadline day.'

He starts belting on the keys again but when he feels my eyes burning into the back of his head, he spins his chair around and faces me.

'Look, if you're desperate for something to do, go see Andrew. He's bound to have a job for you. And I just thought of one, too – you can bring me another cup of tea on the way back – ta.'

It's becoming very clear why he has to buy his own presents. He's not a shark, he's not a guppy – he's a pig.

I knock on the editor's door.

'Yes?'

'Er. The Shark said' – I feel so stupid saying that – 'you might have some work for me.'

'It's quite possible. Let me have a look.'

He peers around his desk. At least I think it's a desk. It might be just one ginormous pile of papers.

'Ah. A press release from our beloved mayor. Burkie's

always after some free publicity.' He looks it over and then pushes it towards me. 'Probably a thousand words in that. Cut it down to five pars. About a hundred words.'

I stand there, staring pathetically, trying to get him to read my mind.

'Any questions?'

'No . . . not really.'

He frowns. 'Pars are paragraphs.'

I nod, probably too many times.

'When you finish, print it out and bring it over. I'll have a look at it, see if it's up to scratch.'

'Okay, Mr Matthews, er, Andrew. Thanks.'

As soon as the Shark is fuelled up again with tea, I attack the press release – hacking away mercilessly. In only half an hour I get it down to seven hundred words. After an hour I pare it right back till it's impossible to lose even another full stop.

'It's about five hundred words.' I stand in front of Andrew's desk. 'Hope that's all right. I know it's more than what you wanted but I couldn't cut out any more. I don't think anyone could – but I fitted it all into five pars, like you said.'

Putting on his glasses, he reads my effort for at least three seconds, then drops it back on the desk and focuses on his computer as if I'm not there.

This is sooo infuriating. SAY SOMETHING! I scream at him.

Mentally, of course.

And then, without even looking at me, and very softly, he does say something.

'Do it again.'

That's the same response he gives to my next two attempts.

DO IT AGAIN!

On the third rejection I flounce back to my desk and flop down as noisily as possible, mad as hell, and utterly defeated.

The Shark turns and raises an eyebrow.

'What's up with you?'

'I can't write this stupid press release. No matter how I do it, it's wrong – it's always wrong!'

'Give me a look at what you've got there.'

'Okay.'

He reads it quickly then screws it up and throws it in the bin.

That's it! I quit! I'm outta here! They're only thoughts but they're an instant away from becoming words.

'Quick lesson.' He spins his chair around to eyeball me. 'You paying attention?'

'Ready when you are.'

'Write this down: who, what, when, where, why, how. Got that?'

'Who, what . . .'

'When, where, why, how. Got it now?'

'I think so.'

'Those are the details the reader needs to know. What happened? Who did it? When? Where? Why? How? Your job is to tell them; most important things first. Keep it simple. Stick to the facts. Joe Blow out in the street, he doesn't want a novel or a play. He wants his news served up in a nutshell. You with me?'

'Yep.'

He turns back to his computer and starts typing again. 'Have another go at it. And keep at it till you get it right. Take the rest of the day if you have to. You don't get good by accident, darl. You work your arse off. Just depends how much you want it – or if you want it at all. Do you?'

'I want it – a lot.'

'In that case, no more moans and groans – we agreed?'

'Yes – and thanks for helping me.'

'Now just one more thing before you get back to work.'

'Cup of tea?'

'Thought you'd never ask.'

I start a fresh page in my notebook. Up the top I write in capitals: WHO, WHAT, WHEN, WHERE, WHY, HOW. I try to remember the rest of the stuff he said, too. Keep it simple. Lots of facts. News in a nutshell. Okay. I can do this. Brand new start. I rewrite it, switch the paragraphs around, tighten it up. Shine every single word. At twelve o'clock I go for lunch and take the press release with me, reading it over, making sure I've nailed it. At five minutes past one I hand it to Andrew. A minute later he pushes it onto a spike on his desk. That's all.

'Must have liked it,' the Shark says.

'How am I supposed to know? He didn't say a word!'

'But he didn't throw it back at you. That's usually a good sign.'

CHAPTER 18

'I DON'T THINK I WANT to go back to that job tomorrow, Bull. It sucked.'

He mutes the TV and looks up. 'Tell me about it.'

'For a start I wasn't a journalist – I was the tea lady.'

'Bet you were good at it, too.'

I ignore him and head into the kitchen to make a sandwich.

'Don't go spoilin' your dinner, Tiff. It's not far away.'

'Can't wait, Bull. Dying of hunger.'

He switches the sound back on.

'Thought you wanted to hear about my day?'

I hear him groan and the sound goes off again.

'Go ahead,' he says. 'Tell me.'

I decide on pancakes – and toast. As I'm cooking I give Bull a running commentary on my newspaper adventures. Our house is tweeny and my voice isn't. I know he hears every word.

'They've got some geriatric there who's the main reporter. I say hello and he goes, "They call me The Shark." It's because of the way he gobbles up stories or something – I almost burst out laughing when he said it. I'm like, "What are you on?"'

'The Shark, eh . . .'

'He's so deluded, Bull. He really believes he's this hotshot reporter, when he's not even a has-been. He's a never-was.'

'Sounds like a character, all right.'

'But even more stupid was Andrew – he's the editor. He wants this story cut from a thousand to a hundred words, right?'

'Right.'

'That's really hard to do. I get it to seven hundred, five hundred. Each time it's not good enough. I get it to three hundred. He goes, "Do it again."'

'Must have been a pain.'

'It was! Then on the fourth time, at last he doesn't say to do it again. But he doesn't say "it's good" either. He just takes it off me. Not a word of thanks, Bull. Nothing!'

'Well . . .'

'And the day just dragged like torture. It was so boring.

But the worst thing was that they really didn't want me there. I was in the way.'

He doesn't respond so I stroll back into the lounge room with my food. His eyes are glued to the TV.

'Bull, have you been listening to anything I've said?'

'Bits and pieces. I got the gist of it.'

'Excuse me?'

'Keep your hair on, Tiff.'

'No! I always listen to your stories about work! No matter how boring they are!'

'Look, it's not that I don't care – I do. Truly. But your timing's all wrong. You barge in and start this blow-by-blow account when they've got the footy highlights on TV.'

'Thanks a lot, Bull!'

'Aw, fair go. It was a State of Origin match.'

I'm standing there, staring and fuming, wondering if I could get off on justifiable homicide, when I hear footsteps behind me.

'I was listenin'. Heard every word.'

When I turn I see Reggie, looking like he just crawled out of bed.

'Hi, Reggie. I didn't wake you, did I? I might have got a bit loud.'

'That's all right, Tiffy. Wasn't asleep. Just had a lie down. I been feelin' a bit weary on it lately.'

His face looks grey and pinched, as if the skin has been

pulled tight against the bones. Then I realise, with all of my 'me, me, me' ranting, I completely forgot about his doctor's appointment.

'I'm sorry' – I give him a hug – 'for not asking about your day.'

'Not a problem, luv.'

'How did it go with Anna?'

'Ah, you know what doctors are like. They got no idea of privacy, like she says, "Now Mr Bennett, how have your bowels been?" So I ask her how hers have been – see how she likes it. I mean, that's a bit below the belt, isn't it?'

Bull splutters out a laugh. I keep mine inside.

'Anyway,' Reggie continues, after a glare at Bull, 'she wants me to have all these blood tests and x-rays and God knows what. You go through all this stuff and at the end of it . . .' He sighs and leaves the rest unsaid.

I tell him for about the hundredth time that he'll be fine and he agrees with me – both of us trying to make the other believe.

Bull puts a hand on Reggie's shoulder. Not a word is spoken. They hardly look at each other. They're so awkward about getting close, and yet somehow they make it.

'Now, about this newspaper business.' Reggie's voice crackles with an energy that he didn't have only a moment before. 'Here's what I reckon, Tiffy.' He inches half a step forward and Bull moves his hand away. It's as if they've both agreed that they've had their share of closeness for now – at least the kind that's visible. 'You're bein' put to the test, luv.'

'How do you mean?'

'Seems fairly obvious to me. This editor joker went all out to make it tough for yer. If you don't front up tomorrow, then you failed the test. Give it another go, Tiffy. One more day.'

I really don't need a lot of persuading. Yes, it was awful writing that press release and getting no feedback from Andrew about what I was doing wrong, and no thank you when I finally got it right. I won't be forgiving him in a hurry. But I don't mind the Shark all that much. He's grumpy and rude and sexist. But at least he did try to help me . . .

I give Reggie another hug.

'It's not me birthday, is it?' he asks.

'No. That was for the good advice. Here's the deal: You'll have all your medical tests this week and I'll go back to the paper – and I'll take anything they dish out. We'll be tested together, Reggie.'

'You're on, luv.'

CHAPTER 19

I RING KAYLA AND REHASH the Shark story – think I'm still going to be talking about that when I'm old and feeble. By the time I hang up I feel happy from all the laughing – but then Zoe arrives. I haven't got anything against her, of course, it's just that Bull promised he'd give me a driving lesson tonight. I know the promise is worthless now.

'I only called in to see how Reggie's doing,' she says. 'I don't want to interrupt.'

Whenever she comes over, Bull drops everything to spend time with her. They'll probably watch a movie or listen to music or just talk. Whatever they decide, it's the end of my lesson.

'Hey, mate.' Bull sidles over to me. 'I know I was going to take you out in the car tonight, but I can't.'

'Doesn't matter,' I say. 'I'd forgotten all about it.'

'Got all this paperwork I have to get through, but I–'

'I don't care, Bull.'

'Let me finish. I mentioned it to Zoe. She's game for anything – hey, Zoe?'

It's the first time that I've felt her trespassing on my territory. Maybe Bull put her up to this to try to get us closer. Maybe it's her idea. Or maybe I'm just paranoid. In any case I don't have much choice because in a second she's right here, beside me.

'I'd love to take you for a drive, Tiff. Be good to sit back and get driven around for a change. If it's all right with you, that is.'

I smile.

'Sure, Zoe. Thanks.'

We've got the windows down, front and back. Zoe drives a ten-year-old Magna. It's aircon is in pieces on our garage floor. Reggie's in the process of repairing it. He used to be a mechanic – could fix anything. He's still not too bad, but he's slow and there's always something to distract him. Most days he potters around with the Falcon. It was a wreck when he had it towed home. He's had it sprayed and upholstered, and all the dints have been hammered out. The car takes up most of his time. And when he's well enough he goes to bingo at the Royal. Then there's his old movies and *Dr Phil*, and long, dawdling rambles with Wolfie. And sleeping. He does a lot of that. So Zoe's aircon might take a while yet.

'You drive good,' she says. 'Look, I haven't even got my fingers crossed.'

'Thanks.'

'But I am praying,' she adds.

We've rarely had any time alone together but now that we've got it I don't know what to say. Possibilities keep flying at me but I bat them away just as fast.

I know I can't say these things:

Bull won't tell me your age but you have to be at least forty or even more. I can't imagine being that old and not being terminally depressed, but you seem to be putting on a brave face. Go, girl!

Have you had lots of boyfriends? He won't tell me that either.

Do you want to marry Bull?

WHY?

Okay, none of my business.

I think he'd be in it. He likes you. I'm sure you know that.

If you married him, what would happen then? Would you move in with us? Would Bull move out? I know those things worry Reggie. It isn't personal. It's just the whole change thing

– it scares him. I think it's rubbed off on me a bit . . .

A few minutes later Zoe breaks the silence.

'How was working at the paper? Did you like it?'

There's a lot I could say, but I manage to sum it up with a nod, and just one word. 'Yeah.' I figure that should cover it.

She looks at me and laughs.

'Did I say something funny?'

'Well, yes, you did as a matter of fact. It got me remembering when I was your age. Whatever my parents asked me, I would try to answer in one word. Or a shrug was even better.

'What did you do at school today, Zoe?

'Schoolwork.

'Who was that boy you were talking with?

'Shrug.

'From when I was about fourteen to seventeen, maybe eighteen, my parents must have thought I was a spy, or an alien. I wouldn't tell them anything and I would rather have died than be seen in public with them. And they probably felt the same way about me. At one stage I had three colours in my hair and a lip ring, because I knew that would drive them insane!'

Smiles really are contagious. I catch Zoe's from her. It feels kind of special being with her and talking like this and laughing and – is that something up ahead?

CHAPTER 20

'ROO!' ZOE SCREECHES. 'BRAKE! Brake!'

I jam my foot down till I'm almost standing. The brakes squeal and the car pivots and slews to the left. Zoe reefs at the handbrake but momentum propels us on, metal grinding and shuddering till we stop. The car is side-on and plum in front of a tree. Behind us a kangaroo hops off into the scrub.

'Sorry! Zoe, I'm sorry!'

'It's okay. It's over now. No damage.'

'It just jumped out from nowhere!'

'That's the worst thing about night-driving in the bush. Things can happen so fast.' She lays a hand on my forehead. 'You're so cold. Shaking a bit, too. You got quite a shock.

So did I. Just straighten the car up and pull right off the road for a minute. We both need to catch our breath.'

I do it.

'Better put the hazard lights on, too. We don't want to be rear-ended.'

I do it.

'Crazy roos.' She turns around to try to see if there are any more. 'Been here six months and I've been called out to five prangs caused by roos. The damage they do. Cars written off. People smashed up. There was one fatal, too. Bull might have told you about it, that one over at Gudden. A big red went through the windscreen and into a car. The driver made it – I don't know how – but the old guy in the back seat wasn't so lucky. The truckies have got the right idea: drive right over the top of them. Don't swerve like we just did because that's when . . . Tiff?'

I struggle to open the door but can't make it in time.

Push my head through the window.

Spew my heart out.

CHAPTER 21

'I'M SO INSENSITIVE. RAVING on about accident scenes and here's you in shock.' She wipes my face with a handkerchief.

'I'm so sorry, Zoe.' Can't look at her. Feel like I'm about to die from embarrassment.

'Come here, you big dope.'

She suddenly leans in to hug me. It's a perfectly natural thing for her to do, but I still pull back.

At the same time I hear myself telling her, 'I've already got a mother.'

I don't know where that came from. It's just there and I say it in such a cold and cruel way.

She pauses a moment to take that in, to recover.

'Yes, sure,' she says. 'Of course. I understand.'

But even I don't understand.

We sit for a moment, the night breeze a whisper on our faces. I'm certain she's trying to work out what to say next. I am too.

She thinks of something first.

'I'm a very good listener, Tiff. If it was an Olympic sport I could listen for Australia. So if you ever want to talk about anything – here I am.'

'Thanks, Zoe. Maybe some other time.'

'Not a problem . . . well, it's probably best if we call it a night . . . unless you feel like driving again.'

I've got my head down, my eyes closed – but she keeps on trying.

'Get thrown off, get straight back on the horse, that's what they say, Tiff. I think it might be a good idea, but if you don't want to . . .'

'Okay.' I look up at her. 'I want to.'

I slot in behind the wheel and head the car for home. My nerves are still jangly and I go slower now, my foot poised near the brake, just in case. All the time I'm trying to unknot my thoughts so I can explain them to Zoe. But they're tangled-up fishing-line thoughts and I can't undo them. Maybe if I just talk I'll be able to blunder my way through.

'What I said before – I didn't mean to hurt you.'

'Don't be silly. You didn't hurt me. Tough as old boots, I am.'

I keep my eyes trained on the road, but the tone of her voice tells me she's most probably smiling. Zoe is one of those hard-to-knock-down people – or maybe she just bounces back really well. She's sunny no matter what the weather, and obviously brave, since she gave me another shot. Forgiving, too. It's the way I've always imagined my mum would have been. If she had lived she'd be about Zoe's age now. It could have been us out here. I coast along with that thought for a few kays, don't want to turn it loose, but I know I have to let reality back in. Sometimes I hate reality.

'Watcha thinking?' she says.

Here's my chance to really let her see me and all my mixed-up feelings . . . if only I knew where to start.

'Not much. Just looking out for roos.'

CHAPTER 22

I DIDN'T GET A LOT of sleep last night. That suicidal kangaroo gave me nightmares. Once I woke up in a panic – hanging onto the sheets and pushing down with my foot to hit the brakes. I fell back to sleep and lapsed into the same dream. Suddenly the windscreen shattered and a roo came at me head-first. Reggie was in the back seat.

By then I was too afraid to shut my eyes. I lay there and let my mind drift. All I could think of was Zoe and what I'd said to her. My mum is always with me, but I hadn't realised how deeply I felt about her until the words actually came out. It must have sounded so screwed up. I wonder what she thinks of me – what she told Bull.

Most mornings Reggie sleeps in late. That's the way it is today at breakfast; just me and Bull, and Wolfie, of course. Where there's food there's the Wolf.

I talk first.

'Hope I didn't freak Zoe out too much last night. She say anything to you?'

'Nuh.'

'I almost got us both killed, Bull. She must have said something.'

'Well there was one thing . . .'

'Go on.'

'She said you'd be a terrific driver overseas.'

'Why overseas?'

'They don't have kangaroos there.'

Pleased with himself, he tosses Wolfie a piece of toast.

'Don't make fun. I'm being serious. I was pretty shaken up after the roo and I might have snapped at her . . . I did snap at her. She didn't mention that?'

'Listen. I got no idea what you talked about with her. All she told me was that she hoped she could do it again – go out drivin' with you. She likes you, Tiff. I've tried to talk her out of it, but I can't.'

'Aw. Okay. Thanks, Bull.'

'Too easy. Now can you get out of the way of the TV?'

CHAPTER 23

IT'S MUCH MORE LAID-BACK at the *Eagle* today. The paper's been printed and everyone's got a copy on their desk. They sit around reading it like it's some fantastic best-seller. Like they're all little William Shakespeares – even the ad reps – and they've just cranked out another work of genius. The Shark and Jordie are smiling to themselves, patting each other on the back. Come on. Get over it. I flick through the thing in about ten seconds. The *Eagle* is so deadly dull.

Andrew moseys over, the paper in his hand. He drops it on my desk and returns to his office without a word. A story is circled in red pen. I take a closer look . . . it's only small and it's buried in a corner, that's why I missed it before. It's that press release about the mayor that Andrew kept getting me to rewrite. The *Eagle* has suddenly got interesting. My name's under the story! I've scored a by-line!

'Thanks!' I stand outside Andrew's office, pressing my story up against the glass. He looks up from his computer, nods, raises his thumb, and then continues typing.

Back at my desk and desperate to share my news, I tap the Shark's arm.

'You rang?'

'Check this out. My first story. My first by-line.'

He sighs, like it's a really big effort to look at it. It's then that I realise I'm the only one it matters to. Should have just kept it to myself.

The Shark gives it a swift once-over.

'Not bad, not bad. That's one down. Only a million to go.'

'Right. Thanks, Shark.'

I should have known to expect something like that from him.

'Now that you've proven yourself I reckon you've earned a go at a very important assignment.'

'Making tea?'

'No, I said important. You want to have a crack at it? '

'All right. That'd be good.'

'That's the way. Run down the post office and get the mail for us. Key's hanging up in the front office. When you come back I want you to open it up and sort it into three piles: good stuff, bad stuff, and shit. Off you go.'

You bastard, Shark. You bastard. I say that to myself as I trudge away.

'Oi. There's one more thing.'

I turn to face him.

'It wasn't the greatest story in the world by a long chalk, but I saw you there, working at it. You tried hard. Did the best you could and didn't give up. One thing I know: Andrew doesn't hand out by-lines unless they're deserved. So well done. Now pick yourself up, girl. It's a good day.'

I'm buzzing after the Shark's little speech, but it wears off as the morning drags by. Andrew goes to his editors' seminar – probably for the rest of the week – and the Shark's too busy to talk to me or can't be bothered. All I do is open mail and make tea and wonder why I ever thought I'd like working here.

Then Joan Maxwell arrives. Nancy told me I'd know her when I saw her. She's right. Joan's a large lady with a jolly smile – someone's favourite aunty, or maybe their grandmother. I like her immediately.

'You must be Tiff. Hello. I'm Joan.' She looks at the wall clock, shaking her head. 'That can't be the time.'

'I think it is, Joan.'

'Oh, rats. I'm running late. I struck every red light. And

now I need to go to the loo. I didn't want to go at home when I had time. But now I do. Why do our bladders play these mind games?'

I can't think of an answer to that, but I'm in luck because she doesn't want one anyway. As soon as she says it she rushes off to the toilet, only pausing to yell out to me before she turns a corner.

'When I come back I'm going off to an interview. Like to join me, dear?'

I look across to the Shark for permission.

He nods. 'Think I can scrape by without you.'

A few minutes later I'm in Joan's car. She's driving, and chatting.

'I work three days a week, Tiff; interview people, do profiles, features, the social pages – who got married, who died – the nuts-and-bolts of life. The Shark calls them "fluff" stories. I suppose he's right. Mind you, he thinks that about any story that doesn't involve a body count.'

This morning we're on our way to meet Clarence Dawkins. The only thing that makes him newsworthy is that today he is one hundred years old.

'Next week he'll be on the front page of the *Eagle*,' Joan says. 'God I hope he can hang on till then. If he dies we'll be really stuck.'

I search her face for some sign that she's kidding. There isn't one.

We arrive to find the street packed with cars – so many that Joan has to drive around the block twice before we find a parking spot. Inside the house there are balloons and glitzy decorations, a heap of cards strung together along a wall, a chocolate cake with what has to be a hundred candles, and a continuous slide-show with photos of the birthday boy. His whole life is up there: from when he was a baby, to a school kid, to the army, to marriage and family, on and on till today.

Clarence is sitting in a plush red leather chair with a handful of people clustered around him, all speaking very loudly so he'll hear.

'The journalists are here from the *Eagle*,' one says. 'We better let them do their job.'

A path magically clears before us. Power of the Press. I like it.

'Morning,' he croaks. 'Pleased to make your acquaintance.'

Clarence is a shorty. I have to look extra hard to convince myself he's not shrinking in front of us as he talks.

'It's a pleasure to meet you.' Joan gestures for me to move closer, which I do. 'And this is my young friend, Tiff.'

I want to tell him that he looks like he's in good shape for someone who should have been dead twenty years ago, but I give it a miss. Some people don't know how to handle compliments.

'Hi.' That's all I say.

'From the newspaper, eh?' He peers at the business card that Joan gives him. 'So I suppose you want to know all about my life.'

'Oh yes. Very much. I've been looking forward to it.' Joan is so polite. 'That would be lovely.'

I hope he's not planning to give us the day-by-day version.

'Let's see now.' He tilts his head back and plays with the dangly skin flapping on his neck. I've never seen anyone do that before. Not even a turkey. 'I still do my exercises every day. Eat lots of spinach and cabbage. Always been very fit. If you know what I mean. Very capable. Still am.'

He arches an eyebrow and looks at Joan like a sex-charged tortoise, before leaning forward and resting a hand on her knee. Joan watches in stunned amazement as his fingers tiptoe up her leg, along her thigh – oh-my-God! She pushes her chair way back and jumps up, all flustered and fluttery.

'Now, now, Clarence.' She waggles a finger at him. 'I think that might have been just a little naughty.'

They both smile. It's full-on embarrassment with Joan. With him it's good old-fashioned lechery.

We're there for another half an hour before Jordie arrives to take photos. It's a perfect excuse for us to leave. In that short space of time Joan's captured Clarence's life in her notebook, at least the part of it that anyone's interested in. There's only one more thing to ask.

'How did you get to be so old, Clarence? What's the secret?'

'Got no idea,' he says. 'One breath after the other. Keep on doin' that, you get there.'

It's incredibly dreary, but he's a hundred so it's still newspaper gold.

We start to make a run for it.

Joan says, 'So good to meet you. It's been quite an experience.'

I say, 'Happy birthday.'

'Hang on, lass. There's something I want to tell you.'

He waves me closer. Joan frowns, her meaning clear: Stay away, stay away. I go over to him anyway. I figure a real reporter would.

'Yes, Clarence?'

I feel his dry lips brush my ear and then hear his gravelly whisper, 'I'm only ninety-eight. Keep it under your hat.'

'Okay. I will.'

As soon as we're out the door Joan wants to know what he said.

If I tell the truth Clarence might never get his front page. And yet I don't want to lie. Think. Think.

'Tiff?'

'If it's all right with you, Joan, I'd rather not repeat it.'

'Oh goodness me.' She nods and sighs and gives me a consoling pat on the back. 'I was afraid it would be something like that . . . the silly old goat.'

CHAPTER 24

FOR A FEW MINUTES over dinner I get a taste of what it's like to do stand-up. I tell Bull and Reggie about Clarence and his wandering hands; and Joan jumping up and looking horrified; and how he's really ninety-eight, not a hundred. I time my punch lines just right and the laughs crash over them like waves.

I also work in a mention about my by-line, brushing over it like it's not important, hoping they'll think it is.

Bull: 'You got your name in the paper? Already? Jeez, that's not bad.'

Reggie: 'Did you bring it home for us to have a look at?'

Me: 'I'm not sure . . . I think I might have one in my room. I'll check.'

The truth is I've got five copies; thought I'd stock up just in case I never get another by-line.

Bull reads every word out loud. Reggie looks on over his shoulder. They both say they're proud of me. Like the Shark said, it's a good day.

Reggie goes to bed early.

'Love yer, Tiffy.'

He's saying that more now than he ever has. I catch his hand and hold it for a second.

'Love you, too.'

Bull grabs his keys. 'Goin' up to see Dan at the servo. Won't be long.'

I block his way. 'How come you never say you love me?'

'Savin' it up.'

'What for?'

'Me deathbed.'

I look around for something to throw at him, but he strikes first, picking me up like I'm nothing, whirling me around and then dropping me down on Wolfie's beanbag. He stands over me grinning like a lunatic.

'Night, mate.'

'Night, Bull.'

We must have had a thousand moments like this, being together and happy. Not one of them stands out from the rest. I suppose it's like eating chocolate. You love it at the time, but after you've licked the last trace from your lips, it's just gone.

I turn on my computer and write about today in my journal, so I can keep it.

CHAPTER 25

I'M TEN OR FIFTEEN minutes into my journal catch-up when Kayla texts me.

'TIFF! NEED TO TALK. CAN U COME UP?'

I phone her straight away.

'Yeah, sure, I'll be there . . . hey, are you crying?'

'I was trying not to. But nothing's wrong, well, yes it is—'

'What's going on, Kayla?'

'It's complicated. There's really good news about Colin and Inky. But there's something else I have to tell you – about us.'

'Us?'

'I need you to be here when I tell you. Face to face. You coming up, Tiff?'

'On my way.'

I hear Bull come home and race out to catch him before he drives into the garage.

'Need a lift up to Kayla's. Okay?'

'What happened to being nearly eighteen and all that Miss Independent stuff?'

'That was then.' I jump in beside him. 'Something's wrong with Kayla. She was crying on the phone and not making any sense. I have to be there – now.'

Bull drops me outside her door.

'I'll come in with you if you like.'

'No offence, but Kayla just wants to see me.'

He taps his phone. 'When you're ready to come home, give us a shout.'

'Door's open. Come on in.'

Kayla's not the only one who's been crying. Inky has too. She and Colin huddle together on the yellow lounge. No sign of the kids.

'Where are Rowie and Harrison? They all right?'

'Asleep,' Kayla says. 'They're fine.' She hugs me like I've just returned from a long trip, or I'm about to go away.

'Will someone please tell me what is–'

Colin interrupts. 'We're getting married, Tiff. Me and Bess.'

Inky bawls her eyes out as if it's bad news from the doctor; like she's got Terminal Matrimony. Colin holds her in his muscly butcher's arms and rocks her side-to-side.

'And I didn't even have to ask him,' she says. 'He wants to do it because–' A fresh stream of tears get in the way and Colin has to finish the sentence for her.

'It's because I love her.' He says it loud and strong, not afraid of the words; proud of them. 'Took me time working it out. Weighed it all up, knew this was right for me. Bess and the babies, Kayla, little Montana just around the corner; family, it's what I've always wanted.'

'Now do you know what I mean?' says Kayla. 'How could I tell you all this on the phone?'

Can't argue with that. This definitely needed a personal visit. And a few extra boxes of tissues.

'Well done, you two!'

I go over for some hand-shaking. That's good enough for Colin, but not Inky. She pinches my cheeks together like she's moulding play dough and plants a sloppy kiss on my nose.

'I've never been married before,' she gushes. 'I don't know what I'm supposed to do.'

'Whatever I tell ya.' Colin grins wickedly.

Kayla's eyes widen – I think she's about to whack him one.

He puts up his hands in surrender. 'Only kidding.'

Inky looks fragile. Kayla takes her in her arms and shoots me a look that says: 'Help me out here.' So I join in. We're a couple of blotters soaking up her mix of sad and happy. Colin stands back watching us, looking proud and glad, and when he blows his nose, all of us laugh, because he sounds like a honking duck. It's a stand-out moment that I'll remember for a long time, but I have a feeling there's something else waiting for me, as if this is one of those good news, bad news stories. Okay, I've heard the good part . . .

'Kayla, you said on the phone this was about us, too.'

She nods. Colin takes Bess by the hand.

'We should leave the girls alone to have a talk,' he says.

'There's nothing to worry about.' Inky rubs my arm. 'Everything's going to turn out for the best.'

Hold on, I've seen this movie. That dialogue is straight from a scene where the condemned guy is being led to the electric chair by the prison chaplain. Whenever anyone says there's nothing to worry about, you can be sure it means the exact opposite.

Inky and Colin go into their bedroom and shut the door. Kayla sits beside me on the lounge. She takes a deep breath and begins.

'Tiff, I'm really, really sorry – I never wanted to say this, hate it so much, but I know it's going to be all right–'

Is she deliberately trying to torture me?

'Kayla, will you please just get to–'

'We're leaving Gungee. Colin's got a house for us – in Perth.'

Well, I knew this would happen. Right from that very first day on the bus when we were kids. I've never been very good with people. Don't know why I ever thought it would change with Kayla. If I was meant to have a sister then I would have just had one, without any wishing or hoping, without any of this.

'Fine. Cool.' That's what I say. 'When you going?'

She stares at me, her mouth open.

'Don't you even care, Tiff?'

Sometimes words just don't get you there . . . don't let you say all the stuff from deep in your heart, stuff that no dictionary has a name for.

I head for the door.

'Where are you going? Come back in here and TALK to me. Tiff!'

A light rain is spitting outside and there's a wind raking up the leaves on the driveway as I run down to the road. Kayla's behind me, talking, talking. It only makes me run faster.

'You are not going anywhere' – her hand falls heavily on my shoulder – 'till we sort this out.'

I stop but can't bring myself to face her.

'I do care.' I say it to the road. 'You know I do. I just care too much. That's a problem I've always had. People like me, we've got no halfway – we take life too seriously and we get hurt and . . . Kayla, you're my *only* friend.'

'Hey!'

She stands in front of me with her hands wrapped around mine. I can't avoid her eyes now.

'How long have we known each other, Tiff? Eight years? Ten?'

I could tell her the very day we became friends. I wrote it down because I had a feeling it would be important. But if she doesn't know, I don't either.

'I'm not sure,' I say. 'Something like that.'

'Well I'm just starting to get used to you – I'm not going to give up on us now.'

'But you'll be in Perth. Not a train ride or a bus ride away. Perth. That's like another country.'

'They've got email there. They've got Skype. We can still talk every day. And it's not like I'll never see you again. When we're little old ladies we're still gunna be hangin' out together. We'll always be friends, Tiff. Don't you know that by now?' She's all sniffles and drips. Her chin is shaking.

Yeah. I know it.

'I'm sorry, Kayla. I didn't mean to hurt you. It was just a shock and I got sad . . .'

'Well get un-sad, you big dope!'

The clouds open up and there we are in the middle of the road getting soaked, but not caring.

CHAPTER 26

I'M ON THE BUS to Menindah. There's barely a roadside puddle to show for the downpour and now the sky is powder blue. And the ten or twelve people on the bus, same ones as yesterday, are dressed for cool and comfort. My head is in a book – what a surprise – but I have to give it a rest for a while. I love Sylvia Plath, but I can only read her poetry in short bursts; stay too long in her world and the gloom seeps through by osmosis.

The poem I read before I shut the book was 'Mad Girl's Love Song'. Cool title. The first line gives you a clue about her style. It's about how the world drops dead when she shuts her eyes.

Sylvia killed herself at thirty.

Tempting fate, I shut my eyes too, and as I do last night comes zipping back to me, easy as pressing rewind.

We ran to my house, yelling over the top of the rain.

'I KNOW WHAT WE CAN DO, TIFF.'

'WHAT?'

'SLEEPOVER. JUST LIKE WE USED TO.'

'NOOO WAY!'

'COME ON — OUR VERY LAST SLEEPOVER.'

'WE'VE ALREADY HAD IT!'

'LET'S HAVE IT AGAIN!'

'NEWSFLASH, KAYLA — WE'RE TOO OLD FOR THAT.'

'NEWSFLASH, TIFF — WE'RE DOIN' IT! OKAY? — OKAY!'

Bull opens the door to two drowned rats.

'You should have rung me. I would have come and got yers.'

'That's cool,' says Kayla. 'You can take us back.'

'Thanks, Bull.' I peck his bristly cheek as I brush past. 'Won't be a sec. I'll get some dry clothes.'

'But you just got here.' His face glazes over with confusion.

'I know you're getting old,' I tell him. 'But try to keep up.'

'I'll do my level best.'

'Tiff wants to have a sleepover.' Kayla catches a towel I

throw her and starts drying her hair. 'I couldn't talk her out of it. She's such a child.'

The bus jolts over a pothole and I look outside to get my bearings. A sixty kay sign tells me we're approaching another fly-speck on the map – a few bumps later and it's behind us. Still a long ride to Menindah and the *Eagle.* I tilt my head back on the seat so the sun's rays warm my face. And I close my eyes and go back to last night...

We sit around Kayla's computer while Colin hunts for his flash drive.

'He's got a stack of photos of the house,' says Inky. Her eyes have never looked more alive. 'You just wait till you see it, Tiff – it's lovely. Col, where have you got to?'

'Almost there. Don't get your knickers in a knot.'

In a minute he's at the door, holding up the flash drive like it's a rabbit freshly plucked from a hat. And then the house appears on the screen. It's just another house to me, a lot bigger than the current one, but it has to be fifty years old. It needs paint and repairs, while a couple of grenades would be a good way to start a garden make-over. And it's not really in Perth. It's in Valna; a country town. But as Inky is quick to point out, 'Valna is bigger than Gungee.'

That wouldn't be hard. There are garden gnomes bigger than Gungee.

'I was brought up in that house,' Colin says wistfully.

'Had some good times. My grandparents raised me. Now my dad's got a caravan and he's doing the grey nomad thing around Australia. Didn't want to leave the house empty, so . . .'

That's why the rent is free and the lease is long.

'We'll do the place up real nice, Bess.' He puts his arm around her. 'It won't take long to get it back to how it used to look. Be pretty all right, I reckon.'

Inky plants a kiss on Colin with enough energy behind it to light up Gungee. If it was on TV Reggie would dive for the remote to change channels. He's not into the mushy stuff. Turns his stomach, he says.

'Yuck,' groans Kayla.

Colin flails his arms and legs about as if he's being smothered, but he's still in no hurry to get away. I think it's just possible he might be having a very nice time.

Not too much later Kayla and I are on our own. We each sip a mug of hot chocolate, with marshmallows on top, compliments of Inky.

'Hot chocolate always tastes better with the lights off,' Kayla says.

Don't think so. The only thing that changes with hot chocolate when you turn the lights off is that you're likely to spill it. But I feel guilty for having such a killjoy thought, so when Kayla flicks the switch I say, 'You're right, that's much better.'

And then we're sprawled on the lounge-room floor, all snug in blankets and pillows and whispers.

'I think I'm going to stop calling her Inky.' The house is asleep. There's only Kayla's hushed voice and nothing else. 'Yeah. I've decided. She deserves better. From now on it's Mum – and you can call her Bess – okay?'

'Sounds good.'

'She's never been as happy as this, Tiff. It's perfect. Colin's even lined up a job in a butcher shop. And when they're married and they've got the place looking just right, they'll apply to get Cody and Hales back from their foster homes. Inky – Mum – wants that so much. Me too.'

I remember when the kids were taken away. Bess used to drink a lot more then – that was before Colin. She was always a good mum but she forgot to pick Cody and Hales up from school once or twice and someone put in a complaint. Welfare came sniffing around and didn't like what they found. They've been gone for over a year now. All that time both Inky and Kayla have been scared Welfare would take Harrison and Rowie, too. Colin being there is probably the only reason it didn't happen. Now it looks like it never will.

'They've got an RSL club in Valna, Tiff.'

'Uh-huh.'

'Colin knows one of the supervisors. He's going to put in a good word for me to get a job – maybe waiting on tables in the bistro. I can handle that. Colin thinks I've got a real good chance.'

'That's the *best* news, Kayla.'

'Thanks. I know it's really not all that great, but I'd be glad to have it. And there's a college where I can do an art course. Bistro at night, college in the day – that's how I hope it works out.'

'It will.'

She looks at me, smiling.

'We're not leaving for a few weeks.'

'That's good.'

'So we can still go on our trip.'

I think I know what she means – I hope – but I pause, to let her say it.

'Surfers Paradise – see your mum's grave. You still want that, right?'

'I thought you'd forget – especially now.'

'Thanks for the vote of confidence. Are we still on?'

'Yes. Absolutely.'

The last of the hot chocolate gone, I roll over onto my side.

'Night, Kayla.'

For a moment the answer is silence, and then –

'I didn't want to go to Perth. Dead against it at first – it's so far away. It wasn't doing art at college that changed my mind – I found out about that later. It was Cody and

Hales, and knowing how bad Mum needed them . . . we're a family. You understand, don't you, Tiff?'

'Yeah, I do.'

CHAPTER 27

'SHARK!' JORDIE RUSHES INTO the office, camera bag slung over his shoulder. 'We got a story. A good one.'

'That right?'

'Just got a tip from a cop. Dead chick in the park. Only young. We gotta be there, man.'

One second the Shark is on the phone telling jokes, the next – 'Call you back' – the phone is banged down and he's up off the chair and reaching for his notebook.

'About time something happened round this hole.'

'You're not wrong.'

'Let's do it, Jord.'

I hunker low behind the computer, for once happy to be ignored. The Shark stops at the back door of the office and turns, his eyes hunting me down.

'You serious about this job?'

'Of course.'

'Then this is your lucky day. We've got a hard news story for once. If you're really genuine you should be over here right now. Well?'

Jordie drives fast, the Shark beside him. I'm in the back, full of dread at what might be waiting for me. The Shark looks agitated, leaning forward a little in the seat like he wants to jump out and run ahead, like he can't wait.

We reach the park in fifteen minutes. Near a grove of trees are two green patrol cars and an ambulance, its back doors open wide.

'There she is.' Jordie points ahead.

The Shark squints into the distance. 'Where?'

'See the ambos?'

'Yeah.'

'She's behind them. Between the cop cars.'

'Aw, right. Now I see her. We're in business.'

I make out a small orange-coloured shape on the ground. The dead girl. She's covered over with a glossy plastic material; could be someone's garbage.

Jordie pulls out a camera and drops his bag at my feet. 'Mind this, will ya?'

He's on his way before I have time to reply, running to the girl. The Shark hobbles behind him as fast as his bad hip will allow. Never in my wildest dreams is this what I signed on for. I wanted it safe. I wanted a kindly, patient teacher. And I definitely did not want anything to do with dead people.

The Shark swings around. 'Are you comin' or what? Make up your mind right now.'

I hurry after him as if I'm caught up in his slipstream.

Ahead of us Jordie closes in on the girl, taking photo after photo until two police shoo him away.

He hustles over to us. 'Couldn't see her face, but I got the back of her head, her hair and that – nice arty shot of one of her hands – sort of reaching out, you know? Reckon I might have a front page there.'

'Good man.' The Shark shuffles on, ignoring the young cops who chased off Jordie. They're one-stripers: Constables. Bull's a two-striper: Senior Constable. The older man leaning against one of the cars is a three-striper: Sergeant. Just before he reaches him, the Shark stops and turns to me.

'You bring your notebook? Got a pen?'

'Yes.'

'Righto. Get it all down. What I say. What he says. Don't

worry about word for word – just get the guts of it. You can write it properly when we get back to the office. One other thing: keep your trap shut while you're out here. Not a word. Understood?'

'Understood.'

He takes the remaining few steps. 'Morning, Peter. Lovely day for it.'

'Sharky.'

'Got the headline all written up. *Killer Strikes. Police Manhunt Begins.* That sound about right to you?'

'You wish.'

'Then put me straight, Pete.'

'It's no big deal, mate. Sorry to spoil your day. Just another dead druggy.'

'Aw, right. So there's no chance that–'

'Someone did her in? Nah. Highly unlikely. She was a victim of circumstances, that's all: eighteen and no brain. Only lobbed in town from Melbourne a week back. First night here she goes and does the same as this – bloody OD. We dragged her off to hospital and they got her going again. She was pretty close to dead that time, too. I gave her the lecture myself. Really poured it on heavy. Doesn't look like she learnt much, eh?'

Jordie falls in beside us as we trudge back to the car.

'Go all right, Shark?'

'Waste of time – junky.'

'What a rip off! Had some good pics, too.'

'More wallpaper for your toilet, son.'

I've never seen a dead body before. It didn't freak me out like I thought it might, probably because I stayed well clear of it. All I saw was the piece of plastic on the ground from a long way off. There'll be no nightmares for me. I escaped . . .

The only thing is that now, as I stare out the car window, I can't shake that image from my mind. The body. It's there on the glass as if I'm looking at a TV screen. And if I look really hard – and I do – I see underneath the plastic. The girl's face. Not some gruesome zombie. Just an ordinary girl. Could be me or Kayla. And all of a sudden I feel ashamed that I've been calling her 'it'.

'Kind of quiet in the back there.'

The Shark takes charge of the rear vision mirror – Jordie doesn't seem to mind – and adjusts it until our eyes meet.

'You can ask questions if you want,' he says. 'It's the only way you're ever going to learn anything.'

'Do you still want me to write the story when we get back?'

The Shark laughs quietly and shakes his head. 'I'll let you explain it to her, Jord.'

'There is no story, Tiff. All we've got is that a body was found in the park. We don't really have a drug problem in town, but young kids passing through – you know how it is – sometimes they make mistakes. The cops always say the same. *No suspicious circumstances.* Can't see any headlines there, can you? About as exciting as watching paint dry.'

I don't understand, and the Shark sees it in my face.

'It's like this,' he tells me. 'We can't even say it was an overdose till an autopsy makes it official. Can't say her name till she's identified. She's not a local so God knows when that'll be. News is *now*. By the time we get all the info we need, it won't be news anymore, my friend, it'll be *history*. Couple of pars, that's all this is worth. If that.'

I look at the window again. The dead girl stares back at me. The Shark swivels around in the seat to face me.

'Tell me true. You don't have the stomach for this, do you?'

I'm an expert at hiding the truth when I need to, and I need to now, because I really want this job. But even so, I can't stop the word from rolling out.

'No.'

The Shark nods as if he's known it all along. Nods with contempt. That gets me angry and the anger is stronger than my fear of him.

'You don't care about that girl. It doesn't matter to you that she died – that she has a family somewhere – that she was only eighteen. I don't know how you can be like that, Shark. But *I* can't.'

When he turns back to the road it feels like a door is being slammed in my face. He doesn't waste another word on me.

CHAPTER 28

We're at our desks again side by side, but there's a wall of ice between me and the Shark.

I swallow my pride. 'Is there anything you'd like me to do?'

He crinkles up his nose, shakes his head just once.

A while later I try again.

'I'm going out to the urn, do you want a–'

'No.'

I wish he was openly hostile with me, then I could fight back. But I can't do anything with just 'no'.

It's at least another half-hour before he speaks.

'Andrew won't be in today so you can't get any work from

him, but Joan'll be here after lunch.' He taps away at the keyboard as he talks. 'She'll probably have something for you.'

'Right.'

It's a storm and I should keep my head down, let it blow over.

Should.

'Maybe it would be better if I just wasn't here.'

He lets the words settle for a moment, continues typing, making me sweat it out until I can't take it any longer.

'Just tell me. Do you think I should go?'

He keeps bashing on the keys, harder and faster as if he wants to drown out anything I might say. I talk louder.

'Well, I've admitted I can't hack it and I'm pretty certain you're not happy with me, so I don't know what I'm doing here.'

He stops typing and whirls around to face me, his arms folded.

'I'll tell you what you're doing. You're stoppin' me from working. This isn't daycare. I'm not paid to wipe your nose.'

I wanted him to be angry and he is – his wild eyes burn into mine – but now I'm not able to be angry back at him like I thought I would be. Because I refuse to let him see me cry.

Have to get out of here.

'Where do you think you're going?'

'Home.'

'That'd be right. Run off to Mummy as soon as it gets a bit hard.'

'I haven't got a mummy! She's dead!'

That shuts him up.

I slump into the chair again, my back to him.

It's stalemate for a moment and then he shoves a box of tissues in front of me.

'No thanks. Don't need them.' I push them away.

'Please yourself.'

There's another frosty wave of silence, and then . . .

'First thing: you were wrong. I care about that dead kid. Course I do. It's a waste and it's bloody sad. But no matter what you or I say or think or feel, it's still not a story. And that's what we're here for. In case you forgot. I told you first day: this is a newspaper!'

I reach across for the tissues. Grab a handful. Hide my face in them.

He doesn't talk, but I hear his exasperation loud and clear – it's wrapped up in a worn-out crumpled sigh. I can only guess that his anger got hoisted up on that sigh and carried away, because when he finally does speak again, his voice is even and calm and all the spiky edges are gone.

'Got a stack on today,' he says, 'so I can't spend any time with you. That's nothing to do with this mornin' – I'm just flat out with Andrew being away. So this is what you do.

Take a wander to the post office – grab yourself a coffee if you like – catch your breath. Come back, sort out the mail like I showed you. That'll take you up to lunchtime. After lunch you go out on a job with Joanie – she's always got something planned. The day's bound to improve. They usually do. You don't give it away because of one tough morning. You hang in there. All right?'

I nod. And sniffle.

'One final thing: you're spot on about me not being happy with you – don't know how you ever figured it out – must be psychic. You gotta toughen up or you just won't make it. But don't worry. I haven't written you off yet – not quite. I've got rules. There's one that says everyone gets a second chance.' He taps my arm with his pen. 'We'll give it another try tomorrow, you and me. New day. Clean slate. What do you reckon, we good?'

When I look at him my eyes are probably red, but I'm not crying.

I tell him we're good.

CHAPTER 29

'TIFF?'

It's Nancy on the office phone.

'Yes.'

'There's someone out here to see you.'

'Be right there.'

'Wait.' She whispers the next part. 'Hope you haven't been up to any mischief.'

'No. Why?'

'It's the law.'

When I go out, I find Zoe waiting for me. I know immediately that there's nothing wrong with Reggie or Bull: her smile tells me that. So what's she doing here?

'Had to drive out this way for work. I was only a few

clicks down the road so I thought, seeing I'm so close, might as well swing by and see if you want to have lunch. My treat.'

I could sure do with some company, and a free lunch is always hard to resist. But not for a minute do I believe that she's turned up by chance. She wants to tell me something.

She's moving in with us.

Bull's moving out to be with her.

They're getting married.

They're splitting up.

No, she looks too happy for that.

Maybe she's pregnant!

I hope the baby hasn't got Bull's big head.

'I'm starving,' I tell her. 'Let's eat.'

I'm the vegetarian pizza. She's the fettuccine with garlic prawns.

Zoe is very big on food talk.

'Oh, this is so good. Yum. What's the pizza like? Can I have a bite? You gotta try these prawns. Wish I had the recipe. They're de-lish.'

There's a lot more, too, but she doesn't say it all in one chunk; it's sprinkled in with her comments about passers-by. That's why she wanted to sit at a table out in the street. She's into people-watching. Says it's the best free show in town.

'Is that a wig?'

'He's too old for her.'

'No one wants to see your navel, darling. Especially while we're eating. Put it away.'

In between all that she manages to squeeze in a question for me.

'How's your morning been?'

I skip past my run-in with the Shark and concentrate on the girl.

She nods. 'I heard about that one. Some of the guys at the station were talking about it. So young . . . it's a hard way to kick-off in journalism. You okay with it?'

'No problems.'

She studies my face carefully, trying to work out where the truth is, but I assure her that I'm all right and she drops it, and then picks up a new subject.

'Before I forget, I bought something for Reggie.'

She takes a DVD out of her bag and gives it to me: *McLintock!* A John Wayne movie.

'It was only a few dollars. I saw it in a shop and thought he'd like it, especially being in colour. Could you give it to him for me?'

'Sure, but why don't you bring it over yourself and watch it with us – or do you hate John Wayne?'

She shakes her head. 'I don't hate him. Don't know the first thing about him.'

'Then come over.'

'No, Tiff. It wouldn't be right. You get in some ice-cream and chocolate – watch a movie. It's a family thing. I don't want to barge in on that.'

And it's precisely because she doesn't barge in, that I want her there.

'Hey, Zoe, if you supply some of that ice-cream and chocolate, you can come over every night of the week.'

I hand back the DVD.

'We'll expect you about seven.'

Her meal done with, she glides a spoon leisurely around a coffee mug, not stirring it, just gliding for something to do, waiting for the right second, to say this:

'To tell you the truth I really *wasn't* working out this way.'

Knew it!

'Bull told me about Kayla leaving. I'm sorry, Tiff. I know how close you two are. That's why I called in. Wanted you to know I'm here if you'd like to talk about it – any time at all.'

'You came all this way – for me?'

'Don't be ridiculous! It was for the food. I've heard good things about this place. You were just an afterthought.'

Thanks, Zoe.

'I expected you were going to tell me you were moving in with us.'

'Good God, no. Do I look that desperate?'

I almost choke on my orange juice. She aims her finger at me like a gun and smiles.

'Maybe one day that could happen,' she says. 'If you and Reggie were okay with it. I'd ask you first. But there's no rush. We're trundling along just fine the way we are. But getting back to you, since I'm here – you want a talk?'

'What about?'

'Whatever you got – I'm not fussy.'

I've always told Reggie and Bull what's going on in my life, but mostly they get the outside layers. That works best for them, and for me. My secret thoughts and feelings are shared with just Kayla, my journal and Wolfie. They're all very good listeners, although Wolfie spoils the mood sometimes by chasing a flea right in the middle of an earth-shattering disclosure.

But now Zoe is here and willing, and it feels right.

'Well, it's like this . . .'

It's easy enough telling her about Colin and Bess's good news, all the excitement of the new house and the possibility of Hales and Cody leaving their foster families and coming home. It gets tougher as I move on to Kayla going to Perth.

'Always knew we'd go our separate ways one day,' I tell her. 'But it still took me completely by surprise.'

There's a skill in knowing when to meet someone else's

eyes with yours, and when to look away. I'm glad that Zoe has mastered the art, so I can blink out the speck of dust in my eyes. Ask anyone who knows me, I rarely do tears. But today, with the Shark, and now here, those specks of dust have been a real nuisance.

'The thing I've noticed about life–' Zoe pauses to drain the last of her coffee and lick the foam off her lips, 'is that it just keeps coming at you. And it can be a real bummer. What you need to remember, Tiff, is that you're not alone. You've got friends and family. That's how we get by. We talk and share and eat cake and giggle in the dark, even when we're scared – no, especially when we're scared.'

Wow. Reggie would be really impressed. She's as good as Dr Phil. And not bald.

'You'll get through this,' she says. 'You and Kayla will still see each other. Jump on a plane and you'll be in Perth in no time at all.'

'That's true. And before she leaves we're going to Surfers Paradise, just like we planned – I'm going to find my mum's grave.'

'That should cheer you up!' She immediately slaps a hand across her mouth. Through her spread-out fingers I hear, 'Sorry. That was awful . . . but I couldn't resist it.'

'It was funny,' I say, to her immense relief.

She laughs; not her big uproarious laugh, just a little one, between her and me. 'Tell you what, Tiff,' she says. 'I'll make a prediction – no, two predictions. One: Your friendship with Kayla is going to stay rock solid. Two: Your mobile bill is going to shoot through the roof!'

A few minutes later we stand outside the *Eagle*. It's time for Zoe to leave. I sense her hesitancy. The other night I pushed her away and now she doesn't know how to say goodbye. It's not a hard problem to fix. I make the first move – a quick hug and a simple smooch of her cheek; just the normal way you'd treat a friend.

CHAPTER 30

ON THE BUS BACK to Gungee Creek, I try to write a few lines about the girl in the park. What I come up with is not good – well, okay, it's seriously bad. I cross it out quickly, in case someone looks over my shoulder. All I can do is dig deeper. Have to find the girl I saw when I looked in that car window. I'll keep trying. With a bit of luck one day she might tell me what to write.

'Somehow she should be remembered.'

That's what I tell Bull when I get home.

For once he listens to every word I say, because it means a lot to me and I show it – and he doesn't give me any of that 'just a druggy' stuff.

'If you like,' he says, 'I'll try to get an address for her parents. When you write the poem and you're happy with it, you can send it off.'

I hug him. It takes us both by surprise.

After I had lunch with Zoe, I went out on two jobs with Joan. Now, over dinner, I revisit the highlights for Reggie and Bull.

'My picture will be in the paper next week,' I say. 'Jordie, our photographer, got me to sit on top of a giant pumpkin, while he took photos.'

'That might pose a problem.' Bull rubs his chin. 'How will people know which one's the pumpkin?'

Reggie to Bull: 'Give yerself an uppercut, mate.'

Forging ahead, I move on to the interview Joan did with an old couple, Merv and Eileen.

'They've been married fifty years.'

'Not a bad innings,' says Reggie.

'But not that unusual, either,' adds Bull.

'No, but get this. They didn't marry till they were nearly forty – and they've still racked up fifty years together! I'm seventeen and I'm thinking it's all over because I haven't got a guy, but now I can tell myself I've got till I'm forty. It gives me hope.'

Reggie: 'Knock it off, Tiffy. Some bloke'll snaffle you up long before forty.'

Bull: 'Be a pumpkin fancier, most likely.'

I give him the slow-burn glare. He says, 'Sorry!' but he still smirks away like the naughty schoolboy he'll always be. Poor Zoe. She doesn't know what she's letting herself in for.

There are things about that interview which I'll write in my journal later tonight. Years from now I'll still be sad to read about Eileen, losing the fight with dementia right before my eyes; but it will be good to remember Merv, who held her hand the whole time as she dozed, and called her 'Mum'. I'll remember Joan, too. The story really got to her because her own husband died a few years ago. Through the interview she kept dabbing at her eyes.

'The most important thing I got from sitting in on that story,' I tell Reggie, 'was realising that by the time it was over, I knew more about those people than I do about you. And that's not right . . . so I want to interview you.'

'What, for the *Eagle*?'

'No. For me and Bull – and for you, too, of course.'

'Why don't you just talk to me?'

'I'll do that, too, but I want to make it special. I'll type it all up and get Kayla to take some photos – she'll want to help. I'll do it on good-quality paper. It'll be a one-off, collector's edition book – the story of your life. Please say you'll do it, Reggie.'

I expect some resistance but the answer flashes back in a second.

'Aw, yeah,' he says, casual as can be. 'I'll be in that.'
'Excellent. We'll start on it tomorrow.'
'You're on, Tiffy.'

CHAPTER 31

REGGIE GETS THE RESULTS of his tests back in a couple of days but he's not a bit worried about that now. Tonight he's got a John Wayne movie; it can't get any better.

Zoe is in his good books for buying the movie and he's happy for her to watch it with us. I asked Kayla to come over, too, with her camera. Fine with Reggie. The more the merrier. But there is one condition.

'No one talks durin' *McLintock!*' He gives us each a little piece of the evil eye. 'You wouldn't do it at the Kalatta Regent, and you're not doin' it here – not in a John Wayne, yer not.'

Bull puts up his hand. 'What about snoring? That allowed?'

'Think yer funny, don't yer?'

Bull pleads ignorance. 'Huh?'

Before the movie starts Kayla takes some photos of Reggie. He poses for three or four shots then asks for my opinion.

'You reckon I should put me teeth in, luv?

'Doesn't matter, Reggie. Either way, you're still one pretty cool dude.'

'Righto then. It's settled. No teeth it is.'

Kayla gets every possible combination. Reggie sits and stands. He poses with each of us separately, then together. But he looks most relaxed of all when Wolfie pushes her nose up against him, wagging her tail at the camera.

'All done,' Kayla says at last.

'Thank gawd for that.' Reggie sighs with relief. 'Now let's watch Big John.'

CHAPTER 32

WE'RE NOT LONG INTO the movie when the doorbell rings. Wolfie barks then burrows down in her bed, in case it's a burglar. We don't get visitors at night in the middle of the week. The cop car out the front seems to deter home invaders, so if the bell rings the caller is either broken down or they're lost. There's only one other alternative – John Wayne's ridden in to town.

'I'll get it.' Bull goes out to the door. We pause the DVD and strain to listen as the conversation on the verandah floats back to us. The first words are lost when Wolfie responds to the stranger's voice with a rumbly growl. She tries so hard to be brave.

'Quiet, girl.'

And then it all wafts through to us loud and clear.

'Yeah, I remember you – you're the young smart-arse who tried to take my head off at the footy game.'

'Only because you kicked me.'

'Get real. That was an accident.'

'In that case I punched you by accident. So now we're square.'

Kayla looks at me and mouths, 'Davey.'

I bolt to the door, reverting to slow motion before I get there. Can't look too keen. In fact, must look surprised.

'Oh. Hello.'

'Hiya, Tiffany.'

'What are you doing here?'

'There was nothing on TV.'

I'm not sure how to react. Has to be a joke, right?

He looks back at me perfectly straight and solemn.

It's really hard to force a smile. I don't think I make a very convincing job of it.

Bull opens the door wider. 'You better come inside,' he tells Davey. 'I'll try to explain things for you . . .' With an exaggerated sigh he turns back to me. 'It's a good long drive from Tarwyn, Tiff. You think about it. No one comes all that way 'cause there's nothing on TV. Not even Bonehead, here.'

I can almost hear Davey's thoughts. They're saying: *Aw, no. Now I have to punch him again.*

But before he can launch a blow, Bull redeems himself.

'Term of affection, mate.' He says it with a big puppy dog grin that no one would want to punch.

'What *did* you come here for?' he asks Davey.

'To see Tiffany.'

'Who?'

'Tiffany.'

'Awww, riiight.'

Bull ambles off – dirty big smirk on his face – trying out all the la-di-dah ways he can say 'Tiffany'.

That leaves me alone with Davey. He starts talking first, which is great because I have no idea what to say.

'Had no trouble tracking you down. Everyone knows each other in small towns. I just asked up at the shop.'

So much for the witness protection program.

'Been thinkin' about you for a while now,' he says, 'wonderin' if I should come over, say hello. Couldn't find an excuse till tonight.'

He hands over a package he's been trying to hide behind his back.

'This is my excuse – it's a present for you.'

'Really? How come?'

'Open it. You'll see.'

It's wrapped up in red paper held together by a zillion pieces of sticky tape. I try to get them off without tearing the paper but quickly give up and rip it to shreds.

Breakfast At Tiffany's.

'Sorry it's a bit tatty. It's an old book but the words are still in good nick. I wanted you to have it.'

I know a gulp isn't enough of a reply, but it's the best I can do. I open the book carefully, half expecting I'll be squirted by water or a spider will pop out. This has to be a joke. But all I find inside is a folded-up note.

Tiffany,
I like you but you mightn't feel the same about me, and I wouldn't blame you. To save us both from any awkward moments I've figured out an easy way to do this. Nod if you're even slightly interested in getting to know me. Write me a ten page explanation if you're not.
Davey.

'I spent hours trying to get that right and it still sucks,' he says.

The note is brimming with confidence but I don't see that on his face or hear it in his voice.

'It's hard telling a girl you like her, because you could be making a complete idiot of yourself, as well as embarrassing her. So . . . you don't owe me any explanations, Tiffany, just tell me "no" and I'm out of here. No questions, no hard feelings – *gone*.'

He goes to take the note back, but I pull it away from him.

'Only ten pages?' I raise my eyebrows. 'That's nowhere near enough. I couldn't cover it in just ten pages. I'd need a lot more space to express myself. I could probably fill up a book.'

'You might as well nod then,' he says.

And that's what I do.

CHAPTER 33

WE WALK INSIDE AND find Reggie and Zoe looking normal enough, but Kayla greets me with a wide and taunting smiley face. I shoot her a look that plainly says: Stop gawking. I know it's hard to believe – I'm having trouble with it myself – but it's true. A guy is here to see me. So get your eyes back in your head before you scare him away!

Bull does the intros.

'This is Zoe, Reggie and–' Kayla gets in before he can introduce her.

'We've met. Hey, Davey. I was hoping you might turn up one day. Tiff talks about you all the time. "Davey this, Davey that" – she just won't stop!'

I'm going to kill her!

'I do not!'

He looks disappointed.

'Well, I might have mentioned you once – by accident.'

Bull takes over again. 'You remember him, Reggie? He's the one who took a poke at me at the last Gunners' game.'

'You couldn't have hurt him,' Reggie tells Davey.

Bull takes it as a compliment; puffs out his chest and stands a little bit taller.

'Got a head on him like a block of concrete – nothin' gets in or out.'

Zoe laughs first and loudest. 'Good one, Reggie.'

I'm certain Bull thinks it's funny too, but he doesn't let it show.

'Thanks for the support, old bloke,' he grunts.

'No worries.'

I hold up my book like I'm showing off a gold medal I've just won.

'*Breakfast At Tiffany's* – that's why Davey came over – he wanted to give me this.'

Zoe: 'That's nice.'

Kayla: 'Awwww.'

Bull: 'Should have posted it, son. Would have been cheaper than the petrol.'

Reggie looks longingly at the frozen image of John Wayne on the TV screen, the movie still paused.

Davey bends down to pat Wolfie. 'So is this your dog?'

Please Bull, no smart remarks. But he just can't stop himself.

'Was it the tail that tipped you off?'

Davey grins, gives Wolfie one last rub, and hops back to his feet.

'Is there anything around here to do?' he says.

He must be kidding. It's eight-thirty. Nothing is open. Most people are asleep. Even the lobsters at Chans have been tucked in to bed by now. This is Gungee Creek – the land that time forgot.

'Not really,' I say, apologetically.

'But it's a good night for a walk,' pipes up Kayla.

'Yeah,' says Zoe. 'Top night. It's beautiful out.'

They both look at Davey, and I do too.

'I just got an idea,' he says. 'You want to go for a walk, Tiffany?'

CHAPTER 34

I GAZE BACK AT THE house expecting to see Bull setting up a spotlight on the verandah. No sign of him, or the others. That doesn't mean they're not peeking out from behind the curtains. And why not? If it was Kayla out here instead of me, I'd be peeking for sure. How can you tease someone later unless you've got all the grisly details? I bet the only one who isn't looking is Reggie. He'll be too busy pressing every button on the remote so he can get back to the movie. John Wayne will end up riding his horse backwards, and Reggie will still love it.

We head up the road side-by-side, but apart in every other way. It's so dark I can't even see Davey's face. Surreal, that's what this is. All we need is some fog swirling around our feet and this could be a scene from a creaky old horror movie.

A young girl wanders down a lonely country road with a vampire – a fairly cute one. We see the fear in her eyes, not because she's with an undead dead guy, but because she's terrified she'll trip over her clunky feet and headbutt him as she's falling. If there's a way to screw up a promising scene, this girl will find it.

The movie in my head stops, when Davey speaks.

'I've been thinking about you, Tiffany.' His words are soft, but more certain than before. 'That time you came and talked to me on the bus, you didn't know what kind of trouble you might be walking into. I was in a bad way that day, but it didn't stop you. I don't know anyone who would have done what you did.'

'Nahhh,' I drawl. 'It was no big deal. Besides, I couldn't help myself. I'm always doing wildlife rescues – it's kind of a hobby. When I saw you run off the field, all stressed out like you were, I just clicked into injured wombat mode. Reflex action.'

My words are met by a silence. Somehow I've managed to plant both feet in my mouth, again. Now what? Do I try to explain that he doesn't really remind me of a wombat? Or do I say nothing and just hope a semi comes along and squashes me?

Before I can decide, he takes hold of my hand.

'You don't mind, do you, Tiffany?'

A shock runs through me, being so close to him, so suddenly, but it only lasts a second. It's been a while since a boy held my hand. The previous one would have been Jeremy Thomas in Year Four. I'd just bought him a muffin at the tuckshop, so I was his best friend, for all of ten minutes.

'No,' I murmur. 'It's okay.'

As we walk on he asks me about my life, because, 'I really want to get to know you.'

I break off bits and pieces for him: about Reggie being sick, and Kayla moving to Perth, and books, and poetry . . .

'You've really never heard of Sylvia Plath?'

'Sorry.'

'Don't worry. I'll tell you all about her.'

And working at the paper – loving it and hating it – and Bull being really nice when you get to know him, and Zoe, who's going to make him even nicer.

He listens intently, asks questions.

We keep on going, way past Kayla's house, up to the highway. That semi I'd hoped for a few minutes ago roars out of the night. It shudders by and the wind drags at me. At the same instant Davey curls an arm around my waist, anchoring me to him. I'm no delicate flower; I'm strong and capable and I don't need his help, but I like being so close to him.

He tells me about his three older brothers – two lawyers

and a teacher – and how he tried to be like them.

'More to please my mum than anything else, but I couldn't do it. I messed up bad before I moved to Tarwyn. Couldn't handle uni, so I quit. Had a fight with my dad and got kicked out of home. I was drinking back then. My girlfriend came to her senses and dumped me. She said I was immature. Can you believe that?'

I'm not sure how to answer, but his grin tips me off.

'Oh yeah,' I say. 'I can believe it. It sounds like you were hopeless!'

'I was,' he says, shaking his head, and smiling. 'I was a pain in the butt – to everyone. But all that bad stuff was a year ago. I'm better now – promise. I left Adelaide and went feral for a while; lived rough and wandered; took any job I could get, stayed in lots of country towns before I finally ended up in Tarwyn. I'm a Stop-and-Go guy for the council these days.'

'What? You mean you hold up those traffic signs?'

'Yeah. It's a no-stress job, gives me time to think. Might do something else one day but right now I'm happy with it. But you mightn't be . . .'

'Why do you say that?'

'It's not real classy.'

'So? What makes you think I care about classy?' I turn and look at him even though I can't make out his features. 'I'm not into class, I'm into people.'

He doesn't say a word.

'I've always wondered about Stop-and-Go guys. Do you like it if drivers wave and say thanks as they go past? Or is it better if they ignore you? Most times when I'm out in the car with Bull, I give a wave and a "thanks". Usually the guy with the sign stares at me as if I've just escaped from an asylum. So what's the right thing to do?'

'I've never met anyone like you before, Tiffany.'

'Really?'

'No – never.'

'Then you just haven't been to enough asylums.'

Now even in the darkness I see his face, because it's so very near to mine.

I fit neatly up against him.

Our arms hold us together.

He has the softest lips.

Later, when he drives off, he honks the horn all the way till he gets to the corner. Even after he turns onto the highway, I stand in the middle of the road waving, knowing he can't see me, but just wanting to be close to him for a few seconds more.

CHAPTER 35

I ONLY HAVE TO KNOCK once and the door is whisked open by Bull.

'Get lost, did ya? I was about to send a chopper out looking for you.'

Another half hour and he probably would have, too.

'Thanks for caring, Bull.'

'Who said anything about carin'? Your turn to wash up, that's all.'

Back in the lounge room, Kayla hits me with questions, just as I'd expected.

'Well? What happened? Tell me! Don't leave out a thing – I'll know if you do!'

'Nothing to tell. A walk's a walk.'

'Tiffff! You can't do that to me!'

I'm driving her mad. And loving it.

Zoe sits beside Reggie in front of the TV, both looking relaxed. It occurs to me that at last she might have won him over. She smiles at me, most probably appreciating the fun I'm having, as Kayla tries again.

'Aw, come on, Tiff. I'd tell you. Play fair. You gotta give me something!'

'Oh all right then . . .'

The kiss is not for sharing. I've got it locked away. Saving it for days when everything goes wrong, for nights when I'm lonely, and for old age, when I can barely remember what a kiss is like. Call me greedy, I don't care. It's my one piece of magic.

But I do have some news I can tell Kayla.

'Davey's taking me out on a date. On Saturday.'

'Where to?'

'Rifle range.'

I'm not sure who laughs first. Is it Zoe or Bull? Kayla isn't far behind them. Only Reggie keeps a straight face.

'Don't take any notice of 'em, Tiffy. They're only jealous.'

'Yeah, right.' Kayla grins. 'Wish I could get a guy to take me to the rifle range. That's always been my ambition. Woo-hoo.'

'Sorry to laugh, Tiff,' Zoe says, 'but it does seem like a

strange place to go for a first date. Why there of all places?'

'It's not a *bit* strange,' I tell her. 'Davey's thinking of taking up shooting as a hobby, so he wants to check out the rifle range and he asked me if I'd like to go with him.'

Kayla snorts. 'Are you kidding me? He should be checking you out – not a rifle range! No way is that a date.'

I go to the one person I know I can depend on.

'It *is* a date, isn't it, Reggie?'

'S'pose it all depends on how it goes,' he says. 'If you have a good time, come home happy, then it was a date.'

'Okay.'

'But if he shoots yer, it wasn't a date – it was an ambush.'

'Reggie! That's mean!'

'You know I'm only kiddin', Tiffy.' He puts his arms out and I gladly fall into them. 'Don't worry about what anyone says, luv. It's a date.'

CHAPTER 36

I FEEL THE STORM COMING from the time I leave Gungee to when the bus grinds to a halt one street away from the *Eagle.* The first drops whack against me as Nancy opens the office door. Just as I step inside, rain tumbles down behind me, louder by the second. Everyone in our office stands at the front window and watches. It's like we've never seen rain. Outside, drivers switch on headlights in the gloom and slow to a crawl as gutters overflow and water courses across the road.

When my mobile rings I only just hear it. I move away from the others to answer. It's Reggie. He hardly ever calls me, so my mind is instantly crowded with all the things that could be wrong.

'Reggie. Are you okay? Is everything . . . Hello?'

We can't hear each other so I make my way towards the kitchen where I know it won't be as noisy. Halfway there his voice comes through, clear and strong.

'Yeah, Tiffy. All good with me. I was worried about *you*. Heard on the radio there's been a few accidents with all the rain. Just wanted to make sure you got to the paper in one piece.'

I smile at the phone, wishing Reggie could see me.

'You're all right then, luv? No dramas?'

'Not a one.' I reach the kitchen. 'Thanks for thinking about me.'

'Gotta look after my girl. Only one I got.'

My smile gets even bigger.

'Wanted to talk to you anyway. You got a minute or are you busy? You just say if you are, it's not important.'

As he says that, the rain eases. With nothing more to see everyone will head back into the office and I'll have to be there too. But not yet.

'Never too busy for you, Reggie.' I ease down against the rogues' gallery wall. My photo is up there now. 'I'm all yours. Talk to me.'

'Well, I got some good news for you. Believe it or not, I've almost got the old girl up and runnin' again.'

The Falcon. I never really thought he'd do it.

'Good for you, Reggie! That's excellent!'

'Ta, luv. By gee, I put in some hours on her lately. Worked till late last night. Got up early for once and had another go this mornin'. The Wolf almost drove me mad wantin' me to throw the ball for her, but I still got a fair bit of work done.'

'I hope you didn't overdo it.'

'Nah. I'm feelin' good today; fit as a fiddle. Had to give it up when it rained but that doesn't matter. I know exactly what needs to be done now. Reckon another ten or fifteen minutes, half hour tops. That's all. Finished. Done. She'll be tickin' over like a clock.'

'Fannn-tastic! We'll get some photos of you in the car to go with your interview – you still up to doing it tonight?'

'What interview's that, Tiffy?'

I feel miserable that he's forgotten so quickly, but I've learnt not to show it.

'Your life story. I'm going to interview . . . hang on, Reggie.'

I stand up when the Shark comes into the kitchen.

'Wondered where you got to.'

He's got his cup with him.

'I'm just finishing this call.' I show him the mobile. 'It's kind of important. Can you give me another minute? I'll make your tea and bring it in to you. I'll be quick.'

He puts his cup down and holds up his hands, palms towards me. 'No rush – not if it's important. You carry on. I'll fix this.'

I can't believe it – he's making his own tea! Miracle!

'You want me to get you a brew while I'm here?'

Double miracle!

'No, I'm good. But thanks, Shark.'

He nods, drops in a tea bag, fills his cup with hot water and a drop of milk, and traipses off again.

'Sorry, Reggie. That was my boss. I have to get to work.'

'Aw, right. Of course. You go, luv.'

I can read Reggie's thoughts, just like he can read mine. There's something going on with him. It's there, written in his voice, plain as. He must be bored today, or lonely, or maybe he's worried about those test results. Whatever the reason, I know he doesn't want to get off the phone.

'It's okay, Reggie, the job can survive without me for just a little bit longer.' I head back to my desk. 'What were you saying before?'

He has to think a moment to pick up the thread. I usually let him find his way, but now I haven't got the time.

'It was about the Falcon, Reggie. You almost got it going and then it rained–'

'Yeah, I know all that. I wanted to tell yer somethin' else. I've been thinkin' about it for a good while.'

As I turn into the office I find that the Shark is looking directly at me.

Please, Reggie, get to the point, finish the story.

'Tell me.'

'All right . . . for a long time I had this idea that I'd get the Falcon goin' and then I'd take off for a big drive – get out of everyone's way for a while – didn't want to weigh anyone down, if I got sick, yer know?'

'Reggie, what are you talking about? That is such–'

'It's hard to work out sometimes . . . the right thing to do.'

'Just ask *me*! Running away is wrong! You've always taught me that!'

'Calm down, luv. I've decided it's not a good plan – that's what I'm tryin' to tell yer. I know you'd worry yerself sick. Couldn't do that to you. So you'll just have to put up with me. I'm stayin' right here.'

'Good! And don't you ever think of leaving us, Reggie. We'll hunt you down if you do – and you'll be so sorry.'

'I'm shakin' in me shoes.'

'You should be, too.'

'Now listen – about the Falcon. I'm not touchin' her till you and Bull get home. I want you both here when that motor kicks over.'

'We'll be there.'

'Good-oh. And you can get some pictures of Bull's jaw droppin' to the floor, too. How many times has that bloke said I'd never get it–'

'I'm sorry, Reggie. I really have to go now. I'll be in trouble if I don't.'

'You scoot then. I'll see yer later. Love you, Tiffy.'

He hangs up before I can say it back to him.

CHAPTER 37

'NOW I'LL GIVE YOU a demo on how we gather news.' The Shark dials a phone number as he speaks. 'First thing you learn in this job is that any kind of extreme weather means you've got a story. Heavy rain like that has to cause damage, right? So you ring the emergency services, find out what's–' He turns his back to me as the call is answered. 'Harvey, me old mate! No, I'm not dead yet, try to be patient. Now, Harv, that was some wild weather we had. Bet your phones have been runnin' hot, have they? Yeah? Yeah? Is that right? You got some addresses for me, chief?'

He frantically scribbles a message and hands it to me. *Flash floods, trees down. Get Jord!*

All morning we trawl the streets, Jordie snapping photos of the debris while the Shark fronts up to distressed householders with his notebook, pen, and a ton of nerve. I gladly obey his order to stick close behind him. I'd hide under his coat if he let me.

The people we meet are all having a shocker of a day. They might have splintered branches strewn across their yards, or a gaping hole in the roof with a chunk of tree sticking out of it like a giant's spear. We find a group of houses where surging water from a creek has swept inside; not deep, but still ruining everything in its path. The owners have already stacked most of their furniture in their backyards, and as we arrive they're reefing up the carpets. It's not a good time to be out looking to have a chat.

Some people are teary and despondent, and others can't believe it. A few are just angry and spoiling for a fight. With anyone. And then suddenly a reporter is in their face with his nosey questions. It isn't the power of the media I feel today; it's the hatred of it.

The Shark gets ignored a lot and told to mind his own business; and sworn at, and voices are raised. But though he's fast getting old, I still see a coiled-up force in him that no one wants to challenge. He brushes off the threats and shoulders his way through to the next person, and then the next, until at last someone gives their name and explains what happened and how they feel. And while they're talking, Jordie freezes time with one click, and they don't even seem to notice. Then we bundle back into the car and find another place hit by the storm, and do it all again.

'We might almost have enough.' The Shark scans his notes. 'Yeah, one more and we're done.'

It's only a handful of minutes later that I see Adiba. She's standing with her dad in front of a car, a fallen tree beside it.

'Stop, Jordie.' I touch his shoulder. 'That girl used to go to my school.'

We jump out of the car and Adiba's eyes light up.

'Tiffney!' She's the only one who ever called me that. 'What are you doing here?'

It's easy to talk to Adiba – she's always been nice – and so I tell her about work experience, and she and her dad tell us about how they were in the car when the tree came down, just missing them.

'Be all right if I grab a photo?' asks Jordie.

'Sweet!'

Walking away, Jordie says, 'That should be a great pic. Might be front page material.'

The Shark gives me a nod. Coming from him, it's as good as having a medal pinned on me.

'Time to pack it in,' he says. 'We've got all we need.'

- - + - -

It feels strange to listen in as the Shark and Jordie talk about their morning's work, like two soldiers reliving a battle. I don't feel part of that at all. And I can clearly see the things that are wrong with what they do: they take advantage of people's bad luck, and go to work on them when they're vulnerable. Yet the storm and all the havoc is news, and they have to get their stories. The main difference between me and them is that they've learnt to distance themselves emotionally from what they report. I can't do that. Nowhere near. I wonder how long it'll take before I learn how it's done . . . And then I wonder if I ever want to learn something like that.

The Shark cuts into my thoughts.

'You did all right.'

'Thanks,' I tell him, half-heartedly.

'You listened, didn't you? Took it all in? Got some good experience?'

'I guess.'

'Didn't run off? Didn't complain?'

'No.'

'Well, I've had 'em do all that. Some of these work experiences you get landed with, they won't even get out of the car. You can ask Jord.'

'That's for sure,' Jordie replies.

'But I didn't really do anything – except talk to Adiba. I

wouldn't have done that if I hadn't known her. I'm too shy to go up to strangers like you do.'

'Most of us start out that way,' he says. 'But every time you go out you'll get better.'

I wish I could believe that.

The Shark finds me again in the rear-vision mirror.

'You know how yesterday we had a bit of a dust-up – about that girl?'

I nod.

'Well, what about today? You were in the thick of things. How'd you go? Have any problems with what we did?'

'Not really . . . you were just doing your job.'

'Not really.' He says it softly to himself to hear it again, to examine it.

As he does I realise that it sounds terrible. I should have said a flat 'no' and smiled. That would have bought me time to work out how I really feel. But now the Shark swoops on my doubts. His eyes linger on mine, searching for the things unsaid. I can't hide from someone like him.

'Shark?'

'You've got my full attention.'

'The truth is – I'm just not sure if I can be a journalist.'

'Yeah?'

'This is the job I've always wanted but it's not like I thought it would be.'

'And how did you think it would be?'

'That I'd be in the office most of the time – writing stories on the computer. I could probably learn to do that – with a lot of practice. But it's getting out and going to places like we did just now, where people are in trouble – that's where it's hard. I don't know if I could ever do what you did today. In fact, I'm pretty sure I couldn't.'

'So what are you telling me? You want out – is that it? I don't want there to be any confusion. Just say what's in your gut.'

Though I can hear the words in my mind – *I'm sorry, Shark, but I don't think this job is for me* – I can't bring myself to say them to him.

In the end it doesn't really matter, because he takes my silence as an answer.

And he looks away.

CHAPTER 38

YESTERDAY HAD BEEN ROUGH at the start, but I'd patched up my differences with the Shark, and the stories I'd done with Joan in the afternoon had been just my speed. They were fun and they made me think that yes, this is what I want to do. When I left home this morning I was hopeful. Thought I was in with a chance here. And now it's pretty much over.

It's not until ten minutes later, paused at a set of traffic lights, that the Shark speaks again.

'Tiff.'

That floors me – he knows my name.

'Yes?'

'Don't worry. You gave it a good try.'

I feel grateful, and teary. Keep it to myself.

'Okay. Thanks.'

'Just remembered I have to pick up some gear from home,' he says. 'Got a couple of scrapbooks there you can look at if you want. It'll give you something to do this arvo till we work out what's happening with you. Just say if you're not keen.'

I don't want to hurt his feelings.

'Yes, sure. Love to.'

The Shark tries to smile. His smile muscles probably withered away a long time ago through lack of use, so his attempt is stiff and icy. But that only makes it mean more to me.

'You don't mind making a detour do you, Jord? We're not far away.'

'Not a problem, man. You still at the Soldiers?'

'Until they carry me out, son.'

Soon, tucked away in a back street, we find the Shark's 'home'. It's one of those sprawling old-fashioned pubs that always seem to be built on a corner. The Three Soldiers. Down below is the drinking area and above it are rooms to rent, each leading out to a balcony closed in by a rail of wrought iron, dirty brown with rust.

The Shark winces as he gets out of the car – that dodgy

hip of his. 'Be back in a flash.' He totters off like a beat-up old crab. I smile to myself at the thought of him doing anything in a flash.

Jordie unbuckles his seatbelt and slumps back, eyes closed. 'Our new baby, Isabella,' he mutters. 'Poor kid's just started teething. We were up and down to her all night. I'm wrecked now.'

'That's no good . . . so I suppose that means I can't talk to you, seeing you're tired.'

He opens one eye. 'What do you want to talk about?'

'The Shark, I mean, I don't get it. How come he lives here? He said he's been a reporter for forty years. Why hasn't he got a proper home? Where's his family? What's the deal with him?'

'Your guess–' a yawn interrupts the sentence, 'is as good as mine. Known him ten years and he never lets me in on private stuff. As far as I know the only family he's ever had is the *Eagle*. I'd say he was probably a drinker at one stage – they all were, the old breed of newspaper guys – that might be why he's got nothing now. But I can tell you one thing about him – he likes you.'

'You've got to be joking.'

'Dead set. He's showing you the scrapbooks. Do you think he does that for everyone? Nuh. He likes you. Believe it.'

'But why would he?'

'Dunno . . . Maybe it's because you say what's on your mind – even when it's complete crap.'

'Oh. Okay.'

After another few minutes the Shark emerges from the pub clutching two bulky scrapbooks to his chest. I get out of the car and hold the door open for him as he lays them on the back seat.

'Don't feel like you have to read any of this stuff,' he says. 'It's only if you've got nothing else to do. They're a bit moth-eaten and worn, like me. Probably bore your socks off.'

On an impulse I give him a rub on the shoulder. Seems like he might need it.

He juts out his chin, nods, and hauls himself into the car.

CHAPTER 39

BACK AT THE EAGLE the Shark off-loads the scrapbooks onto my desk. 'That should keep you busy for a while.' And then settles down in front of his computer and starts tapping at his usual frantic pace.

I open the first book. The paper is coarse and yellowing and the ink rubs off on my fingertips and leaves them smudged and black. There are stories on house fires and car accidents and council disputes. Nothing that excites me. I zoom from 1986 to 1988 in a couple of minutes – skipping and flicking. But then I feel the Shark's gaze, cold and penetrating. It's only a heartbeat before he turns away, but it's long enough for me to get the message. I am being so dense, so thoughtless. He is sitting right beside me and I'm dissing his best stories, his life's work – and he knows it.

I quickly flip back to the first page.

'Shark?'

'Yeah?'

'There's so much good stuff in these books, I don't know where to start. Got any favourites you can show me?'

'Oh, I can probably find one or two.'

He pushes his chair closer and begins leafing through the pages. A few moments later Andrew arrives and goes into his office. The Shark glances across to him and half-stands. I know that once they talk my time at the *Eagle* will be over. But Andrew picks up the phone, and the Shark stays with me.

'Here's one you'd like. Young Darren – work experience – got him a beauty.'

I look at the photo of Darren: about sixteen or seventeen, curly hair. He has the Shark in a headlock. Both of them are grinning.

Joan walks in with a cup of steaming coffee. 'Good morning, all.' She holds up a doughnut. 'I bought half-a-dozen. They're in the fridge so the cockies won't get them. Help yourself.'

Right behind her is Jordie, munching on a chocolate doughnut.

'You're the best, Joan,' he says before wandering off.

'Hey, Joanie. Do you remember Darren?'

'Oh, yes. Hard to forget that one.'

The Shark turns to me. 'Told him there was a bank robbery. I run down the street with him to the Commonwealth. Get to the corner, grab hold of his shirt, push him up against the wall and say, "You wait here, son. I'm goin' ahead. Don't you move till I come and get you." Then I go back to the *Eagle*.'

For the first time since I've known him, he laughs.

'Darren turned up here about two hours later,' Joan says. 'And let me tell you, he looked very confused.'

'Was he ever.' The Shark nods to himself, his face creased up with a smile. 'He was crooked on me for a while, but he got over it. I made it up to him by getting his mug in the paper – good result all round.'

'Did he become a journalist?'

'No . . . that's rare. Been quite a few years now since anyone went on with it.'

Joan pats my hand. 'But I have a feeling our Tiff will.'

The Shark lets it go without comment and returns to the scrapbook.

'That's Harold Cummings.'

Another photo, this time of a guy in his mid-forties.

Joan clicks her tongue. 'That was so sad.'

'Aw, I don't know.' He keeps looking at the photo. 'Yeah, he died too young – left a good woman behind, three great kids. All that was sad. But he had a fine old life, Harold.

He was a newspaperman, and good at it. That's as much as anyone could hope for.'

'I suppose,' Joan says, but she doesn't look at all convinced.

The Shark thumbs through some more pages till he gets to the story of a plane crash.

'That was a bad business. Five dead. All of them in their twenties.'

'Didn't you get an award for writing that one?' Joan asks.

'Highly Commended: Country Newspaper Awards. That's as close as I ever got.'

'You should have won it. You deserved to.'

'Thanks, darl. It might have done better but we got an ad in at the last minute. They chopped out half my story and put in a quarter-pager from Woolies for cheap pasta sauce and olive oil. The ad comes first every time – law of the jungle. That's the newspaper game.'

'But you still love it, don't you?' I ask.

'Love might be a bit rich.' He closes the book. 'But yeah, I suppose the job has its moments.'

'Well I must get to work.' Joan moves back to her own desk. 'I've got some calls to make. Don't forget the doughnuts.'

'And I better go over and see the boss.' The Shark stands and stretches. 'He'll want an update on what stories and photos we've got.' He looks searchingly at me. 'And any other news I might have.'

A part of me wants to tell him I've changed my mind. I feel like that's what he's hoping to hear. There's so much I like about the job, the people . . .

'Shark.' It's Andrew.

'Yes, mate?'

'Could you come here for a sec?'

'Sure thing.'

The Shark walks across the room. Standing at the doorway to Andrew's office, he turns and gives me a fleeting, regretful look – telling me I missed my opportunity. Then goes inside and Andrew closes the door behind him.

I try to occupy myself by reading some of the plane-crash story:

Witnesses described an inferno and a thick black cloud of smoke that billowed from the wreckage seconds after the crash.

My concentration wanders and I find I'm looking up at the Shark and Andrew. And now they're looking at me. The Shark's probably just told him that I can't cut it. I force myself back into the story.

The pilot was a twenty-seven-year-old Brisbane man with four years' flying ex–

Andrew takes a phone call. It's only brief. He nods to the Shark. And now they're walking over to me . . . and I can't get my eyes off them.

All of a sudden I have a feeling this isn't about the job. It's much more than that. I see it in their faces.

Andrew speaks first. 'Tiff. Your family's out in the front office.'

My family?

'They rang a few minutes ago to say they were on their way. We've been waiting for them. I'm afraid it's bad news.'

Can't talk. Can't think.

The Shark clamps a hand on my shoulder. 'I'm sorry, Tiff. I'm really sorry.'

I run through the office crying and throw myself into Bull's arms. Zoe's with him and she hugs us both. Somewhere in there I hear Bull say, 'It's Reggie', but I already know that and then it's all a blur, what we say and do and how we get to the car. Then I'm in the back seat with Zoe and she's stroking my hair, trying to calm me. It's not working. I'm wide-eyed and gasping and there's thick glass between me and all the words coming from Zoe and Bull. I hear them but they sound faraway and they don't make any sense. It goes on and on like that, being stuck halfway between here and hell, and then I feel the tyres bump over joins in the bitumen and everything clicks into place and I sit up and I'm shivering and I just can't stop.

CHAPTER 40

I'M IN THE FIRST row at the funeral home, flanked by Zoe and Kayla. Bull's in front of us, looking all official in his grey suit and tie. He'd be more at home directing traffic, but today he's directing the ceremony. I know he's nervous.

There are still a few minutes to go before we start; time to play the song Bull picked: 'I Did It My Way'. The lyrics might be corny, but they're not when Elvis sings them.

Tonight we'll be hearing lots from the King, and even more from the Beatles. Bull's bought a new set of speakers for his stereo and hooked up some heavy-duty lights; we've stocked up on meat and finger food and cake. This is going to be the best barbeque Gungee Creek has ever seen. And at exactly midnight we're switching off the lights and all you'll see is–

The music stops.

'Right,' Bull says. 'We all ready?'

I'm not, but like everyone else, I mumble 'yes'.

'Then let's get this show on the road.'

I take a look around and find that the chapel is almost full. You're a star, Reggie.

Davey said he'd try to make it, but he wasn't sure if he could get off work. He's been great. We've been talking and texting heaps. He wanted to come over before now, but for a while there I didn't feel like I could face anyone. No sign of him today. I'm about to turn around when a hand waves at me from one of the back rows. I see Joan smiling. She's driven a long way and she hardly knows me. That really undermines my resolve not to cry.

'The old bloke hated sad funerals,' Bull says. 'He told me if anyone howls, he's gunna come back and haunt them.'

I dry my eyes as fast as I can.

'So don't say you haven't been warned.'

A ripple of laughter rises above the sadness we're all feeling.

'Another thing he didn't want was anyone making a speech about him. So to use his own words, "If you feel like saying somethin' – put a sock in it."'

– – + – –

I think back to the day Reggie died. Wolfie's coat was still crusted in dried mud when Bull and Zoe brought me home from the *Eagle*. We filled buckets with warm water and sponged her down, and all the time she stood perfectly straight and still, even though she usually runs from water.

Earlier she'd slipped into a trench that the council had dug to lay some new drainpipes. We knew about that because Reggie had told Bull when he rang him at work.

Bull had the conversation locked in his head, word for word.

'"The Wolf got herself into a ditch and it was boggy and she couldn't get out and she was startin' to panic."

'I'm sayin', "Take it slow, Reggie. Nice and easy." He's breathless and wheezing like he's got asthma.

'"It's all right now. I got her out. There's mud and crap everywhere but I got her out."

'But how are you, Reggie? You don't sound too good. You want me to come home?'

'He tries to answer but he starts coughin' and then the gasping gets really bad and – and then the phone hits the floor.'

Bull called ahead for an ambulance and drove home with the siren of his cop car blasting. He and the ambos arrived at the same time, but there wasn't a thing they could do for Reggie. The ambos said it was his heart.

Wolfie squatted outside his door with her head tucked

between her front legs. Big brown eyes alert for the door to open.

Bull peers at the checklist he's working from to see what's next. Charlie Dent has just delivered his rousing version of 'Clancy of the Overflow' – another favourite Banjo Paterson poem, and Mrs Muir has recited 'Do Not Go Gentle Into That Good Night' in her soft and gentle way. I helped Bull put the list together, so I know what's coming.

'I want you to take a few minutes now,' he says, 'to remember Reggie: his life, what he was like – well, you know what to do.'

My mind goes roaming again, this time to Gungee cemetery where Kayla and I held our own memorial service two nights ago. We ate crispy-skin chicken from Chans. Kayla drank a lot of bourbon and a little Coke, and I did the same thing, but back to front. We told 'Reggie stories' to each other, and to Monnie and Grogan Nash, and Kayla asked them to 'please, please, keep Reggie safe'. By the time we left I think she was a little bit drunk. Maybe I was, too.

When I open my eyes the chapel is still quiet. I look at the one thing I've been trying to avoid: the coffin.

Well, Reggie, at least you didn't have to suffer a long drawn-out death from some kind of cancer. Bull and I never talked about it, but I think we both thought that's what your test results would reveal. I know I was scared. So glad you beat that one.

One other good thing is that as far back as I can remember, you were loved, by me and Bull for sure, but by so many others, too. And now you're decked out just the way you wanted; in your oddball little hat with the feather in the brim, footy socks and boots, white shorts, the No 1 jersey, and – your most prized possession – the blazer given to you for fifty years' membership with the Gunners.

You're all packed and set to go, Reggie . . . I just wish I could really talk to you.

'Hey.'

I feel Kayla's welcome hand on my back.

'How you goin' there, Tiff?'

'Goin' fine. You?'

'Hanging in there.'

Bull peeks at his watch. 'Right. We have to move it along now. There's only one more thing to do, so if you'd please be upstanding, while we sing a song that Reggie truly loved.'

Dusty strolls to the front of the chapel and acts as conductor for the Gunners' players, past and present, and we all join in as they belt out the club song.

Givva the gun, givva the gun,
Givva the Gunners' try.

In Gungee mud you'll find our blood,
We're Gunners do or die.

It's the most sniffly, weepy, nose-blowing version I've ever heard. Reggie's going to be doing a lot of haunting. He'll have to take the names of everyone here.

We haven't won for fifty years,
But that don't mean a thing,
We're gunna do it one day,
And that is why we sing.

We hear the low whirring of a motor as the chapel's silver curtains are slowly drawn in front of the coffin.

Givva the gun, givva the gun,
Givva the Gunners' try!

CHAPTER 41

Tonight it's like a different year, a different lifetime. Everyone is happy, happy.

The Gunners go to work on snags and steak in an eating display that would impress marauding Vikings. Their wives and girlfriends cluster together at the other end of the table in a kind of Viking women's support club. And both groups laugh, very loudly.

While it's still daylight, the guys form two raggedy teams of six or seven apiece for a game of touch footy on the back lawn. They're still as hopeless as ever, but they're also playing to the crowd; clowning around and running into each other, collapsing in pretend agony. It's all aimed at getting some laughs, and they sure do that.

Not long into the game, Dusty's car pulls up out front. I get a surprise when Joan walks along the driveway with him.

'Hello, Tiff.' She cups both my hands in hers. 'I was going to drive straight home but I got talking to Dusty – isn't that a lovely name? – and we found we had so much in common.'

'Both Virgos,' puts in Dusty.

I didn't know he was into astrology.

'And he's a cat person, too,' Joan adds.

That doesn't sound right to me.

'Didn't you tell me once you were allergic to cats, Dusty?'

He glares at me for an instant, then smiles at Joan.

'It's only the furry ones,' he says.

'The furry ones?' She crinkles her brow as she tries to work that out. 'But aren't they all–'

'Come on, Joan.' Dusty takes her hand. 'Let's get some tucker into us.'

'We'll catch up later, Tiff,' she says as she's half-dragged away. 'Don't let me go before I talk to you.'

At eight o'clock I'm on the verandah with Kayla and Bess.

Kayla: 'Still no Davey. What a rat.'

Me: 'Maybe I should ring him.'

Kayla: 'No! Don't you dare! He's supposed to call you.'

Bess: 'I agree, Tiff. You don't want it to look like you're chasing him.'

Me: 'Yeah, you're right – both of you.'

At nine I sneak into the shed and make the call.

'Jeez is it that late? Sorry, Tiffany. I've been trying to fix the Holden – working flat-chat – that's why I didn't ring. I kept thinking I'd get it goin', but it looks like it needs a new starter motor.'

'So you're not coming?'

'Are you kidding? Last I heard there was free food up for grabs. I wouldn't miss that.'

I let the silence tell him how I feel.

'Hey, Tiffany. If I have to walk – if I have to steal a horse – I'll be there.'

Not long afterwards I'm in the kitchen with Bull.

'We haven't had much of a chance to talk,' I say. 'How you holding up?'

'Seen it better.'

He takes out the bread and starts whacking on the marg like he's laying cement.

'Think you've got enough there, Bull?'

For a moment he closes his eyes. Maybe he's hoping it's all a dream and when he opens them again Reggie will be back.

'Bull?'

He looks up and skewers me with his leave-me-alone stare, and then he goes to the fridge, takes out a tomato and starts slicing, slicing . . .

Wherever he is, I can't get to him.

'I'll catch you later. Okay?'

'Yeah, Tiff . . . later.'

Back outside I get trapped by a gang of maniacs who all seem to have feet as big and agile as house bricks. They're doing some weird cross between line dancing, Irish dancing, and hopping over red-hot coals.

'Come on!' says Zoe. 'This is fun!'

Reluctantly, I join in, and quickly I'm as mad as the rest of them – twirling and laughing, silly and giddy.

Then over the speakers I hear 'Let It Be'.

I couldn't see Kayla while I was dancing, but now as I wend my way through the crowd, not really sure where I'm going, just wanting to get away, she finds me.

'I can't take that song, Kayla.'

'Yeah, I know. Let's get out of here.'

We escape the party and go into my room, Kayla leaving the door open long enough for Wolfie to shuffle in. I sit on the end of the bed and give her a pat. She rests her head on my knees, looking up at me like she knows exactly what's going on.

'I bet that dumb song got to you too, eh, Wolfie? You reckon it did, Kayla?'

'Had to. It got to you, and Wolfie's a whole lot smarter.'

I throw a pillow at her.

'Surfers Paradise,' she says, shoving the pillow aside.

'What about it?'

'The bus leaves at six a.m. I looked it up. In three days time we're going to be on it. Say yes.'

'Kayla, you know I want to go – but isn't that too soon?'

'You've got no other plans, have you? Except to sit around the house moping. Am I right?'

'Probably – but Bull will need me.'

'He's got Zoe. Say yes.'

'Okay – yes.'

'Cool.'

'But I'll have to make sure it's all right with Bull first.'

'Already done that.'

'And he didn't mind?'

'No way. Who do you think is going to drive us to the bus stop?'

'You've thought of everything.'

'Of course. And don't worry about Davey. If he doesn't show, he's a loser – and who needs him?'

'No, you've got him wrong. He's had car trouble.'

'He rang you?'

'Sort of.'

'You rang him. Didn't you?'

'Sort of.'

'Oh, Tiff. I know that kind of guy. Lots of talk but they don't deliver.'

'He'll be here. He will.'

At ten I run into Bull again, this time at the barbie.

'Good night, eh, Tiff?' He's grinning now.

'So you're okay?'

'Me? Yeah, couldn't be better.'

'You weren't before, in the kitchen.'

'Ah, well. Sometimes it gets to me a bit – about Reggie. But I'm back now.'

'Great. Don't go away again.'

Davey has his mobile turned off. Who does that in a crisis? Doesn't he know this is a crisis? I hate him, and the Beatles *and* Elvis Presley – and I've eaten too much cake!

Where are you, Davey? *I need you!*

I kick the toilet door – twice and hard.

'Are you all right, Tiff?'

Oops.

Joan.

I flush, even though there's nothing to flush, run the tap as if I'm washing my hands, and slink out.

'Yes, Joan, I'm fine.'

'Good, dear, that's good. I heard pounding on the door and I didn't know what to think.'

'Really? Pounding? That's funny. I didn't hear it.'

She looks at me suspiciously, but then shrugs. 'Anyway, I've just popped in to say goodbye. Dusty's going to drive me back to town. My car's there. I've had a wonderful time; meeting everyone, and all that lovely food, and the music.'

'Do you like Dusty?'

'Yes. He's good value. I think I might see him again – you never know.'

'Go for it, Joan.'

'Oh, I will. And I'm looking forward to seeing you back at the *Eagle*, when you're feeling up to it.'

'But I don't think I'm going back. I told the Shark I couldn't handle it.'

'Did you? That's odd, because he gave Andrew a very good report about you. He said you had lots of potential. I was there when he said it.'

'The Shark said that? Wow, he is so lucky he isn't here. He'd be so embarrassed if I kissed him.'

'And the paper sent flowers. Did you get them? There was a note with them.'

'We got so many flowers – I haven't looked at them all.'

'Well, take it from me, there's a note from Andrew. He wants you to do another week of work experience so he can evaluate you. But if you don't want to do it, then no one will think any the worse of you.'

'No, no, I want to. It's just that I know I'll never be like the Shark.'

'Now that's just silly. I can't be like him either, but I still get the job done. Be you. I'm sure that will be perfectly fine.'

'Oh . . . okay.'

'You give it some thought, Tiff. I'd love to have you there. We all would.'

'That's really nice. Thanks, Joan. I'll ring Andrew in a day or two. Is that all right?'

'Lovely!' She taps me gently on the cheek. 'Bye, dear.'

Kayla comes straight up to me. 'I just caught the end of that, Tiff. It sounded like it might be good news. What's happening?'

That time back at the cemetery when she got upset with me, got jealous – I remember that now, but I push it aside.

'They're giving me another chance, Kayla, at the paper!'

And she hugs me.

The party ends at midnight. Only a few more minutes to go. Kayla stands with me at the back of the throng. I'm falling apart. She's picking up the pieces.

'Even if Davey came now, I wouldn't speak to him.'

'Yeah, forget him. I'll find you a boy in Surfers.'

'I've had it with boys.'

'Then I'll find you a girl.'

'Shut up.'

Bull has Zoe at his side as he steps up on the back verandah and signals for the music to be turned off.

'Thanks for coming, everyone. Did you have a good time?'

A raucous cheer rises up to answer him.

'Well done. Now in case you don't know, this party was Reggie's idea.'

'On ya, Reggie!'

'I've got to say that I'm a bit narky on the old bloke,' Bull pauses and looks around, 'because the bugger changed his will! Did the dirty on me! I was supposed to get the Falcon but all he left me was his TAB account – with fifteen cents in it!'

The audience loves it – so does Bull.

'But,' he says, 'he did do something right. He left the Falcon to Tiff. Come on up here and get the keys, luv.'

I never expected this. It means a lot to me, much more than the 'thanks' I mumble.

'Reggie's done a good job with the old bomb,' Bull says. 'Awesome job. But I'll tweak it up some more. By the time you get your licence it'll be a red-hot motor car.'

I take the keys, kiss him and Zoe, and then disappear into the crowd as fast as I can.

'Okay now. Last thing we do tonight for Reggie.' Iron man Bull suddenly gets a crack in his voice. Zoe puts her around him and snuggles in close. 'Sparklers – that's what he wanted,' Bull says, only barely getting it together.

Zoe jumps in to help him. 'Have you all got your sparklers?'

We have.

'Then turn off the lights – yeah – everything! Okay. Good. We're all set. You finish it, Bull.'

'Righto,' he says, back in control now. 'Get your sparklers lit up. That's it. Now everybody. Everybody! Give Reggie a waaavvve!'

It would be a fantastic sight from the air: all these twinkling lights swaying back and forth in the middle of a starless night in Gungee Creek.

Kayla grips my arm. 'Hey, Tiff.'

One tiny, flickering beam is heading down the road.

'Looks like a bike . . . what kind of idiot would be out riding a bike at this time of night?'

I run.

Acknowledgements

The writing of *A Straight Line To My Heart* was greatly assisted by regular workshops with my friends, Sandy Fussell, Vicki Stanton, Chris McTrustry, and my wife Di. As always, Maureen (Mo) Johnson, Ann Whitehead and Marion Smith were just an email away when I needed help. I'd also like to thank the talented and friendly team at Allen & Unwin, which includes Eva Mills, Sue Flockhart, Sonya Heijn and Bruno Herfst. I think they're as good as it gets. Another person who falls into that category is my good friend Leonie Tyle. She was the first to read this, and has encouraged me every step of the way. Finally, I'd like to thank my nephew, David Peters. By coincidence, there's a character in this book called Davey Peters. The only similarity is that they're both terrific blokes.